Jim Smith was born in Doune, Scotland. His life's ambition was to become a police officer, and in 1962 he achieved his ambition and joined the Metropolitan Police at Scotland Yard. During his career, he received numerous commendations for his criminal arrests. He was awarded the British Empire Medal for Gallantry by Queen Elizabeth the Second. This was for freeing hostages being held by terrorists.

Jim Smith

The Man Who Cleaned Gravestones

Austin Macauley Publishers
LONDON * CAMBRIDGE * NEW YORK * SHARJAH

Copyright © Jim Smith 2022

The right of Jim Smith to be identified as author of this work has been asserted by the author in accordance with sections 77 and 78 of the Copyright, Designs and Patents Act 1988.

All rights reserved. No part of this publication may be reproduced, stored in a retrieval system or transmitted in any form or by any means, electronic, mechanical, photocopying, recording or otherwise, without the prior permission of the publishers.

Any person who commits any unauthorised act in relation to this publication may be liable to criminal prosecution and civil claims for damages.

This is a work of fiction. Names, characters, businesses, places, events, locales and incidents are either the products of the author's imagination or used in a fictitious manner. Any resemblance to actual persons, living or dead, or actual events is purely coincidental.

A CIP catalogue record for this title is available from the British Library.

ISBN 9781398454613 (Paperback)
ISBN 9781398454620 (Hardback)
ISBN 9781398454644 (ePub e-book)
ISBN 9781398454637 (Audiobook)

www.austinmacauley.com

First Published 2022
Austin Macauley Publishers Ltd®
1 Canada Square
Canary Wharf
London
E14 5AA

Chapter 1

Two bullets from a Browning 9mm pistol fired into my thigh by a member of a London criminal gang. They were attempting to carry out an armed robbery on a bank. This had changed my life resulting in me leaving the Metropolitan Police and the job I had so enjoyed. My life changed forever, or so I thought. Little did I realise the change waiting for me as I holidayed on the Island of Mallorca in the beautiful Mediterranean Sea would be more life changing than I could ever have dreamt off.

Puerto Pollenca in the north of Mallorca has been a magnet for Scots ever since it was discovered by a Glasgow travel agent in the late fifties and I was back again for my twentieth time. The weather was approaching thirty degrees with some ominous heavy black clouds closing in over the mountains. The local shopkeepers had seen all the signs of rain and had already started to bring their outside displays back into their shops as they looked to the sky. I had just sauntered off the promenade into the Carrer de Mendez a street lined with flats occupied by the local shops and bars situated on the ground floor which reminded me of Glasgow tenements; the main difference being the balconies had sunshades to keep out the blazing sunshine. The playground of the local school opposite was full of young children excitingly screaming and shouting, playing all the same games children seem to play in their playgrounds all over the world. The games soon stopped and the screaming turned to laughter when the first clap of thunder crashed above my head immediately followed by a flash of lightning which lit up the already darkened sky, I did not have to wait long before the torrential rain started which soon had rubbish rushing down the gutters. The children were already back in school except for the one boy who took great joy in dancing and stamping in the quickly formed puddles the downpour had made. At her wit's end, the teacher shouted at him to come into class. Soaked to the skin, he ran past her and into the school. She stood in the doorway shaking her head. Every school has a rebel from an early age. He was no exception.

I ran into the nearest doorway, my shirt soaked through. Stepping back into the shop, I allowed a similarly soaked young couple in. As I did so, I found I was in a Salvation Army Charity shop. There was no point in leaving for a further soaking.

I looked around to pass the time. Clothes racks were festooned with second-hand clothing; one corner of the shop was filled with second-hand furniture. Stacked in no particular manner in another corner were second-hand books, looking amongst them I came across Alan Wicker's book Within Wicker's World. Some years earlier, I had let someone borrow my copy and as often happens people like to borrow books and never return them. I picked up the shop copy and put it under my arm. After about ten minutes, I looked out of the shop. The rain had gone off and the sun was back out. I paid two Euros for the book and left. The steam was now rising from the pavements as they dried off.

Little did I think purchasing this book would change my life forever.

I walked back to the promenade and made my way to the Sis Pins Hotel and sat down outside beneath one of the large green sunshades. A waitress arrived, took my order and walked off. She was every bit as stunning from behind as she was from the front. Although I did not want to make it too obvious, I was studying form. She soon returned with a bottle of Fundador brandy, I watched as she poured it over the three ice cubes wedged into the tall narrow glass. Tourists were under the impression that the drinks were never measured. Oh, yes they were, always in a narrow glass; three ice cubes and then the spirit was poured in to the top of the top ice cube. My mixer, American Ginger Ale was poured from the small glass Schweppes bottle; I took a sip and then placed my glass back onto the table. Smiling at her, I nodded and mouthed 'perfect'. She slowly walked off looking over her shoulder as she did so. She knew what I was thinking!

I started to thumb through the pages of Wicker's book, stopping to look at the pictures as I did so. Inside the front cover, someone had written Christmas 1992.

To Mr and Mrs Farquar-Brown,
   Thanks for providing a real HOME for me in Puerto Pollenca and with every best wishes for the future. I look forward to many more happy days with you.
Love,
Nadya.

I continued looking through the book, what a life Whicker had had. Mind you my own hadn't been too bad either. Twenty years in the police at New Scotland Yard, much of the time spent on crime squads. I would still have been in the job if it hadn't been for an 'arsehole' with a Browning 9mm pistol who shot me through the right thigh as I fought with him on a South London pavement. I was part of the 'squad' who had surprised him and his mates as they attempted to rob a security van.

He never stood trial. We had a fight as I wrestled with him in an attempt to get the pistol from him, one punch to the side of my head with his brass knuckle duster fist, and I fell to my knees with my head spinning.

I can still see him as he stood over me wearing a Donald duck rubber mask. He fired two rounds; they buried themselves in my right thigh. I rolled up into a ball pulling my legs up to my chest as I screamed in pain which for some reason died off. He stood above me, his legs apart facing me as he lowered the gun to my head, his finger on the trigger.

"Fuck you, copper."

I did not feel anything. No pain, no emotion just the sounds of his last words ringing in my ears. Not even the sound of his gun just 'fuck you, copper'. This was no Donald Duck under the mask. It was Kenny Barker, one of London's top bank robbers. He was from a North London family. His father and two brothers had never done an honest day's work in their lives. They used a company of bent solicitors who always seemed to be able to come up with the most ludicrous defences and alibis, which the juries swallowed and came back with a 'not guilty' verdict. Some of the time, the juries had been 'nobbled'.

We had a telephone intercept on his house phone. Every time he or his family used the telephone, we heard everything from what pizza toppings were being delivered to them, who was shagging his wife, and did we feel like letting him know? That would have put the cat amongst the pigeons. We knew more about that family than he did. Was he aware his muscle-bound son was a 'shirt lifter' and was pushing more than weights?

I don't suppose he felt anything as two rounds from a police firearms officer's weapon hit him on the side of his head. His mask swelled like an over inflated balloon and it burst open as the police bullet passed through his brain and burst out through the rubber and splattered on the wall of the bank. He fell in a heap next to me. The firearms officer bent down and pulled off the torn Donald duck mask from Barker's face. His face was distorted the blood pouring from the head wound where the bullets had exited taking a third of his face with them.

I looked at him. I felt myself drifting into unconsciousness. Two paramedics were leaning over me as they stretchered me to the ambulance. They kept talking to me in an attempt to keep me conscious, I presume I must have been in shock as I was later told I kept repeating, "Fuck you, copper, Donald Duck's dead."

Donald Duck was dead. How I loved that firearms officer.

I had lost count of the number of times the video recorder inside my head had replayed the events of these few seconds on a London pavement. Sometimes they were in slow motion, other times they were over in a flash. One thing I knew I could not control my brain's video recorder, although mixing with people and the occasional brandy did help.

"Hello, Bob, back again?"

I came out of my trance with a start; I looked around; it was Manolo my friend and local restaurant owner. He leant his bicycle against a tree and walked over. We sat and had a chat about past times. I had spent the past twenty years holidaying in the town and had watched him grow, get married and have a son.

After a while, he got onto his bicycle and rode off.

"See you tonight, usual table." He waved goodbye.

I looked down as Alan Whicker stared out at me from the cover of his book. I picked it up.

As I did so, a letter fell out that was written on headed paper from a Park Lane Hotel in London. I started to read it.

June 1993.

Dear Mr and Mrs Farquar-Brown,

Please help me. I am with some bad men. They have taken my passport and are making me do bad things. It would make my family in the Ukraine very sad. I do not have your phone number. Try to speak to Tetyana, my friend who visited me at your house last summer. You have her telephone number in London I think. Tell her I am in same house in London. I am so frightened. They have hurt so many girls. Some of my friends are gone. I do not know what they do with them. I pray Tetyana is not hurt.

Please telephone her if you can.

Nadya

What a strange letter. I wonder what the family did about her? I read it over and over again asking myself questions and answering myself. I started to assume the worst. With my experience, I should have known better. As my instructor at the Metropolitan Police Detective Training School at Hendon in London 'drummed' into his trainees: "Never assume anything in an investigation."

How old was she? I guessed she would have been a teenager, in her early twenties at the most. What the hell, it was none of my business, or was it? I'm on holiday. Forget it.

Deep down, I knew I couldn't. I am like a junky. I need my fix and this type of thing is what I needed, or was it me just being a nosey bugger? That had got me into grief before. Will I ever learn?

Oh well, time for another drink.

Is that old bird on the other table giving me the eye?

Get a grip, MacInally. She must be sixty; hold on a minute. I'm fifty-five that makes her five years older than me. No way, well then again when I was twenty, would I have turned down a bird of twenty-five?

I returned to her knowing smile.

It's strange what thoughts go through your mind as you sit on your own.

I obviously had impressed her. She got up from the table and walked away ignoring me completely.

I started to read the book but after a few pages I snapped it shut, I knew I was hooked. I had to do something about this.

Who the hell are the Farquar-Browns?

I finished my drink and strolled around the town. The shops were opening as the staff returned from their siesta.

I returned to my hotel and dozed off on top of my bed for a couple of hours.

Chapter 2
Who Is Nadya?

It was about nine o'clock when I sat down in the Tango Restaurant in the Carretera De Formentor, the street that runs about a hundred yards parallel with the promenade.

I sat sipping a glass of Rioja as I waited for my suckling pig to arrive. Luis, the headwaiter, manoeuvred his way through the maze of tables; my meal held high above his head; it arrived with the usual banter and laughter between us.

"Tell me, Luis, do you know an English family by the name of Farquar-Brown I think they live over here?" I asked.

"Let me think about it. I know the name from some place. Enjoy your meal." He scurried off to the kitchen to collect yet more meals.

As I ate my meal, I could not get that letter out of my head. As I continued sipping the Rioja, I puzzled over the letter's contents. This girl, Nadya, was obviously concerned for the safety of her friend Tetyana. Why would any person leave such a letter in a book and then put it into a charity shop? Forget it; I was on holiday, semi-retired from being a P.I. and fed up sorting out other peoples' problems. I finished my meal and pushed my plate forward.

"All done?"

Luis removed my plate.

"Coffee?"

"No, I'll give it a miss tonight. Perhaps I'll see you in the El Casinet bar later." I paid my bill and left the restaurant.

I walked along the seafront watching the holidaymakers enjoying the balmy evening, laughing with their friends with seemingly not a care in the world.

Then again neither did I, any problems I had were self-made, like reading other people's letters.

I nodded to some people I had seen over the past years. I bet they come on holiday and leave all their problems at home; well at least they don't come on holiday and take on other people.

"I am with some bad men."

What did she mean?

I sat in El Casinet. The bar was frequented by mainly young people. There was a strong smell of Cannabis from the smoke wafting out onto the promenade. I was only on my second brandy and American ginger ale when Manolo and Luis walked in. They joined me at my table.

"You just missed Hugo and Sammy; they came in just after you left."

"Hugo and Sammy who?" I asked.

"The people you asked about, they have a Casa in the Del la Font; they know you. You must remember them they always spend the afternoon sitting in the front of the Daina hotel. He tells everyone he was an ex-army officer. He talks as if he is a king."

"I think I know him. He's about six feet tall and smokes like a chimney. His wife has been a bit of a looker in her time but she is now past her sell by date."

Manolo looked quizzically at me. Luis translated what I had said.

The night passed in an alcoholic haze. I made my way back to the hotel.

The following morning, I was having coffee outside the Sis Pins hotel, I tried to put together the last two hours of the previous evening. Who was that stunning dark-haired beauty I had ended up having a drink with? Maria, was that her name? Oh well, ships that pass in the night.

Walking towards me was a couple, both dressed as if going to a society lunch followed by croquet on the lawn. The male spotted me and they immediately made their way towards me.

"Well, good morning, young man. How are you?" He drew on his cigarette reclining his head and closing his eyes as he did so.

"I'm fine; I presume you must be the Farquar-Browns?"

"Yes, that is us, Hugo and Samantha."

I stood up and shook their hands.

"Bob MacInally, pleased to meet you, I've seen you around town over the years."

"Yes, we are becoming quite the locals, but please call me Sammy," she said as she eyed me up and down.

"Pull up a chair, Hugo." I moved one into position for Sammy.

"Would you like a drink, Hugo, Sammy?"

They settled for coffee.

"The people in the Tango were saying you were looking for us. Are you looking to rent property?"

"Oh no, I was trying to look up an old friend of someone in London, a Ukrainian girl by the name of Nadya. I believe she is a friend of yours?"

Hugo sipped his coffee as Sammy answered, "She walked out on us some months ago. I think it was February. Yes, it must have been, all of six months ago. We have not heard a word from her since."

Hugo put his coffee cup down and picked up his cigarette drawing on it yet again, he closed his eyes as if in a trance.

"Lovely young lady, pretty, we are both very disappointed that we never heard from her again. She said she was going off with some people to crew a yacht, haven't heard from her since. Charming young lady."

I looked at Hugo. "A yacht?"

Sammy answered for Hugo, "Yes, it was very large. It was anchored in the bay. Hugo, darling, didn't you say it was too large to tie up in the Marina?"

"Yes, it was very large, must have had a very large crew."

"So you have never heard from her. That's a pity."

"Not a dickey bird," Sammy cut into our conversation.

"Weren't you in the police, Bob?"

"Yes, I was. Took early retirement and went into private investigation work. What do you do yourself?" Hugo answered for her.

"I'm in electronics, old boy. Well must move on things to do people to see." And with that, they both walked off.

I leant back in my chair.

Which one of the two was lying?

I returned to my room and cautiously cut the front message page from the book and removed the letter.

The following morning, I took up my usual position outside my hotel. I started to read Whicker's book. I had only got to page six when my concentration was shattered by the blustering voice of Hugo.

"What a beautiful morning, you know old chap, I do believe this is the best part of the Lord's Day." I looked at him and thought to myself, what a bull shitter.

"Oh of course it's Sunday. All the days seem to go into one whilst on holiday."

"Ah, an Alan Whicker fan I see." And with that, he picked up the book and immediately looked into the inside of the front cover, apparently satisfied or disappointed with what he had seen or not seen. He slowly placed the book on the table.

"Oh well, must press on. See you around, God bless."

He could not wait to leave me. He walked off, in the direction of the Sally Army charity shop. I followed him and watched as he peered into the window, but of course being Sunday morning, the shop was closed.

The following morning, I sat nearby as Hugo returned and watched as he entered the shop. After about ten minutes, he left empty handed.

It was a few days later when I 'bumped into' Hugo again. He was sitting outside the Daina hotel as if waiting for his 'subjects' to pay homage. I deliberately got into conversation with him. It transpired that his company manufactured spy cameras with lenses capable of filming through a pinhole. I, unknown to him had used similar cameras in my work. Hugo was a mystery man. I was convinced he knew more about Nadya than he was prepared to tell me. I strolled along the promenade and found myself at the 'sally army' shop. I walked in.

"Bob."

I looked around. It was the stunning beauty from the El Casinet bar a few nights earlier. Oh dear, I must have had the beer goggles on. She was not so stunning now.

"Hello again, how are you?"

I hoped I had got the correct person; she could not have put on so much weight in three days.

"I'm fine; it was a good night the other night. Do you still want to marry me?"

"Marry?"

"Don't worry; it is only my Liverpool humour. What can I do for you?"

"Last week, I got a book out of here I think the Farquar-Brown woman brought it in."

The assistant looked at me.

"Snobby cow thinks she is the Queen Mother."

"She walked in here the other day, head in the air looking down her shitty nose at me. 'Elizabeth darling, I'm bringing in these books and video tapes for the deprived locals in the Port'. Jumped up cow, most of the Spanish in the Port could buy and sell her. She talks down to people as if they are a heap of shit. It's 'absolutely this and absolutely that and Hugo darling'. Holy shit who calls their kid fucking Hugo. And where the hell she got my name from I'll never know."

"Well, Elizabeth darling, please show me her gifts donated to the port."

"Why certainly, sir, follow me and call me Elizabeth again and sir will get a bunch of fives, its Liz." With that, she swaggered to the rear of the shop complete with her right hand on her hip and her left above her head waving it in a beckoning action. There was a number of books and five VHS video tapes mostly travelogues.

"How much are the tapes?"

"A couple of Euros each and they are not porn, you dirty git. I would think Hugo keeps his 'blues' private. I reckon he was trying to give his maid one. Lovely girl, I met her one night in a bar in town. She was so upset with what he had done to her. She was sobbing her heart out. I tried to find out what had happened. All she would say was she didn't want to hurt his wife; I would not be surprised if that 'tosser' raped her."

At that point, customers came into the shop.

"Sorry, customers arriving. I must go. Take the tapes and pay for them later." I picked up the tapes and walked back to my hotel.

Chapter 3
Travelogues?

At my room, I assembled my video recorder and inserted the first tape; I pressed the play button and let it run. It was a documentary about a trip on the Nile. Pressing fast forward, I let it run as I sipped a drink and watched boats going up and down the Nile at 'break neck speed'.

It was not until viewing the third tape that, when about halfway through, I noticed that the tape had now changed from colour to black and white and was very 'fuzzy'. I pressed the stop button and ran it back to the beginning of the black and white section to watch it at normal speed. It was out of focus but slowly, the picture sharpened showing what appeared to be a bedroom in an upside-down position. Slowly, the camera was turned bringing into focus the inside of a bedroom showing a bed in the centre with a rustic bedside cabinet on either side. There was a tiled floor. It had all the hallmarks of a Spanish bedroom. I did not have to wait long for this to be confirmed. There was then a close up of an eye which moved back from the camera revealing the distorted face of a man. Hugo.

He then walked out of the room looking over his shoulder smiling at the place where the camera was hidden. After a short time, the recording stopped.

There was a short break. The recording resumed once again showing the bedroom apparently taken on a different day as sunlight was streaming into the room. After about thirty seconds, a young woman dressed in a bikini with a towel over her shoulder entered the room. In her hand was a small plastic bottle which she placed on a bedside cabinet. She walked out of view of the camera. Returning naked minutes later apart from a towel on her head tied like a turban, picking up the plastic bottle, she emptied some of the cream onto her hand and then commenced to massage it over her body. Removing the towel from her head, her long blonde hair fell over her face as she bent forward to dry it. Reaching out, she appeared to switch on a tape recorder; the towel then became her dance partner as she waltzed around the room. Eventually, the music presumably stopped as she stood still. This was followed by blank spaces and sequences taken over different days showing her carrying on a normal life style, walking around the room, getting dressed and undressed. The final part showed her fully clothed lying on top of the bed reading a book a fly appeared to causing her some annoyance as she attempted to hit it with her hand. Finally, in frustration, the book was thrown down and she chased the fly around the room trying to hit it with a rolled-up newspaper. It was obvious that this fly's days were numbered. Walking slowly towards the camera, her head and shoulders filing the TV screen, the newspaper carrying hand raised above her head as she moved in for the kill.

Swipe!

The next recording was like a dying bird fluttering towards a tiled floor and landing at a woman's sandaled feet. The camera then started swinging from side to side and then stopped, showing a very quick view of the room followed by a close up of the young lady's face as she looked into the lens. It is then dropped to show a view of the floor again as it swings back and forth. The picture of the floor remained on the screen for a few minutes. It suddenly moves, pans and jerks around the room eventually filming Hugo as he enters the room his hands outstretched in an 'is there a problem' manner. The camera moves horizontally at speed towards Hugo's cheek. There is then a very close up of Hugo's unshaven cheek as it makes contact. It is then pulled back revealing a gash in his cheek with blood running down to his neck. A view of the floor reappears as the camera drops from the side of Hugo's cheek and rests upside down on the floor.

The lenses on these cameras are bullet shaped coming to a point allowing the lens to operate through the pinhole, a very dangerous weapon in the wrong hands.

I started to laugh to myself, as the next view appeared to be Hugo running upside down out of the room holding his face. The recording terminated. *Oh dear,* I thought to myself. *Hugo has been telling me 'porkies'. I'll bet that hurt!*

Chapter 4
Let's Have a Chat

I just stepped out of the local pharmacy into the afternoon sunshine and almost into the arms of Liverpool Liz.

"Hi Bob, I'm glad I met you. I've had that prick Hugo in the shop trying to get his videos back. He says his wife brought them in by mistake. I told him I haven't a clue who bought them. He then went on to say they were his favourites and would pay me one hundred Euros if I got them back, so if you give me them back, we can split the money."

"Liz, I'm sorry. I have only got four the other one got ripped in my machine and was chewed up. I threw it away. I will give you the other four back and you can tell him some one bought it. Meet me tonight in the El Casinet, about ten o'clock."

"Yeah, okay I'll see you then, bring your money." Waving her hand above her head, she walked off.

At ten o'clock when I arrived in, she was already sitting at the bar drinking.

"I have the tapes, sorry about the other one. Here is an extra twenty Euros to make up for the loss. Hit him for a few bob."

"Don't worry I will. There is something about that guy I don't like. He's creepy."

She was getting the same vibes as me.

"Liz, you were saying you thought he had something going with the Au pair?"

"No way would a girl like that have anything to do with him. She was beautiful and what a figure."

In my mind, I had a mental picture of her dancing around the room in the altogether. I had to agree with her although I couldn't say anything.

"I don't care what anybody thinks. I am sure he did something to that girl. I just knew something bad had happened to her when I saw her crying that day in the bar. She looked so lonely sitting there sobbing. She was staring at a photograph in her hands. Eventually, she took it and held it against her chest as she shut her eyes and took deep breaths. I went over and spoke to her; she spoke pretty good English. All I could gather was she wanted to get away from the man at the house where she was working. She showed me the picture she was holding. It was a man and woman with a boy and two girls. She said it was her parents with her brother and a friend. It had been taken some years before. The girls looked about seven and the brother was a little older. It had been taken on a farm. I had to leave the bar early; I really didn't want to as I felt something bad had happened at that villa. What's your interest in her?"

I didn't answer but got another round in.

"You married Liz?"

"I was but then the wheel came off. The guy who I was married to introduced me to drugs and then he was off with some bird he met in a club in town. I suppose that shocks you, Bob?"

"Nothing shocks me, Liz, after years in police."

"You a Bizzy?"

"Retired now."

"I wish I had known you then. I could have given you some work. I was like a lamb to the slaughter when I met him. I was only seventeen. Anyway, that's all in the past."

We did not continue the conversation. Liz left to meet a friend and go clubbing in Alcudia a nearby town. I declined her offer to join them. My days of clubbing were over.

Chapter 5
A Business Deal with Hugo

The following morning, I was at my usual table at the front of the hotel. The temperature was touching eighty degrees. I didn't have to wait long for Hugo to make an appearance. This time, he decided to ignore me and walked past carrying a carrier bag.

"Hi, Hugo, a quick word?"

He looked over to me and made a pretext of having not seen me.

"Oh, good morning, Bob. I did not see you there."

He walked across to me with his arrogant swagger and his stupid smirk.

"I would like to have a little 'snifter' with you on your own, shall we say three o'clock this afternoon on my balcony second floor in the Sis Pins hotel. I have a little business proposition to put to you. I think it will be of interest to you."

I looked at his carrier bag, which he had rested on an empty chair. The top was open; I could see it was the VHS tapes inside.

"Been shopping?"

"Yes, some odds and ends for the villa."

I looked over to the bag.

"Booze I presume. Oh no videos, nothing naughty I hope," I said as I tapped the side of my nose with my index finger.

"Not at all, that type of thing doesn't interest me."

And with that, he picked up the bag and walked off feigning a laugh.

He looked over his shoulder as he walked away.

"See you at three. Do you want me to bring anything?"

"No, I have got everything you will need."

Dear Hugo had a surprise waiting for him at three o'clock. I settled down and started to read my book. I did not have to plan for the meeting. I had dealt with many bits of rubbish like him before. 'Army Officer, my arse'.

As I waited on the balcony, I poured myself a brandy and American dry over the obligatory three ice cubes. As I did so, I saw Hugo standing outside the hotel. I walked down the stairs and through the lounge with its antique furniture and highly polished brass and copper ornaments. Walking out of the cool air-conditioned lounge and into the heat of the afternoon was like stepping into an oven.

"Hugo, old boy."

He looked around and walked towards me, hand outstretched. I shook his hand; it was like a dead fish complete with hand cream. I directed him upstairs to my room. We entered the room. He sat down after giving the room a look of approval.

"I suppose this is adequate and meets your requirements?"

I did not answer the supercilious git but returned his smirking grin.

I poured him a gin and tonic.

"There we go, Hugo, G and T, ice and slice middle cut no pip." He took the glass from my hand and raised it.

"Cheers, old boy, let's hope we can do business."

"I'm sure we can, Hugo old boy. Basically, I want you to give me the telephone number of Tetyana."

Hugo slowly moved the glass from his mouth and placed it on the glass-topped table, removed a cigarette from his gold cigarette case and put it in his mouth. Snapping the case shut, he lit the cigarette from the lighter built into the corner of the case. Inhaling deeply, he leant back in the chair. Bending slowly forward, he stared straight at me.

"What the hell are you talking about, Bob?"

"Well, it's quite simple. I want the telephone number of Tetyana and then we can all return home happy."

"You have brought me here under false pretences. I don't have to sit here and listen to you. Just who do you think you are? You are not in the police now, if in fact you ever were."

"Now let's not go down that road Private Hugo Farquar-Brown. National Service Nineteen Fifty-Five to Fifty-Seven, Pioneer Corps, most of your service at Aldershot. So cut the crap with me about being a bloody Colonel; would you like your army number? Now will you get me her telephone number?"

"You are in breach of the Official Secrets Act having official army records and I will certainly be bringing this to the powers that be in Whitehall when I return to the UK."

I smiled at him.

"Don't be such a dick head all your life. Public Records at Kew old boy, you and everyone else in the army have their records stored there. It's public information. I'll send you a full copy when I go home, if you wish. It only took a call to a contact who did the research for me. Now will you get me that phone number?"

He looked at me still holding his arrogant pose.

"How on earth would I know the phone number of someone I have never heard of?"

"Well, I believe Nadya gave it to you, correct?"

He shuffled about in his chair and took a gulp of his G and T. He lit up another cigarette, inhaled and blew the smoke skywards.

"As Samantha told you, we have not heard from that girl for about six months. How the hell would I know or even care about where she is, or her friend Tety or whatever you called her. I have no intention of sitting here and listening to your frivolous accusations."

He got up, stamped across the room to the door and pushed down on the wrought iron handle.

"Careful, Hughie boy, it's locked."

He walked back to me and bent over the table putting his face close to mine.

"I demand you open that door or I will call the management and the police."

I stood up, our noses brushed together.

"Get your poxy face away from me, you arsehole. Now let me give you some facts. Your wife may not have heard from Nadya for about six months, but you have. In fact, she contacted you no more than two months ago. Now why wouldn't you have told your wife?"

The tan was draining from Hugo's face.

"Another G and T, old boy. After all, I invited you here for a business meeting and it seems to be going rather well, don't you think?"

He did not reply. I poured him another drink and handed it to him. The ice cubes rattled in the glass as his shaking hand took hold.

"I really don't see what my army record has got to do with any of this."

"Well, you see, Hugo, I want that information and you are going to get it for me or I will be having a little chat with the lovely Sammy and bring her up to date with your activities and your little spell in Colchester 'Glass house' you know the army prison. Wasn't that for a little bit of naughty's, holding another man's dick I believe. In the shower if I am not mistaken. Do you want me to carry on?"

"This is blackmail, Bob. You can't do this to me."

"Wrong, I can and I am, now let's talk about your interest in hidden cameras."

"What do you mean? That's my business. I sell covert cameras, I told you that."

"What about the hidden camera in your villa?"

"Now you are talking rubbish. I haven't a clue what you are talking about. You really are going too far this time."

I smiled at him.

"Hughie boy, you really are a chancer. That is a nasty scar on your cheek."

He looked at me totally shocked.

"That was a gardening accident some months ago."

"Hughie, that may well be what you told Sammy but I know and you know that was another of your lies. I've seen your accident in close up. I'm sure you understand where I am coming from, so where is that bloody phone number?"

He stared at the floor sweat dripping off his nose.

"Look I may have a phone number; I am not sure it is the one you want."

"I'm sure it is, Hughie, so what I want you to do is run along home and bring it to me tomorrow morning at eleven a.m."

"And if I can't?"

I shook my head. "You will and if you don't, your dear wife is coming to my film show of the inside of her guests' room at the villa. Since you were the producer and no doubt viewed it many times. I don't suppose you will wish to attend other than to supply the ice creams at the interval."

"You are one bastard, Bob. This is blackmail, and you have stolen that tape."

"Now look here, private 150, I won't give the rest of your army number. You know it off by heart; you would have answered to it at Colchester. By the way, it's not blackmail, that's such a nasty word. It's purely a business deal. And the meeting we agreed to have is now over."

I walked to the door, unlocked and opened it. He walked slowly towards me, head bowed. I put my arm around his shoulder and gave it a little squeeze.

"See you tomorrow eleven am sharp, old boy, bye."

He did not reply.

I kept out of his way that evening; as usual, I ended in the El Casinet. Liz was sitting with some friends from the local shops. We had a few rounds of drinks and eventually her friends left to go to Chivas a local night club.

Liz pulled her chair closer to me.

"That prick Hugo has been to the shop again. He's getting all shitty telling me I must find out who has got the missing tape saying he will pay five hundred Euros if I get the tape back. Did you see what was on it, that he is so desperate to get it back?"

"No, it just chewed up as soon as I put it into the machine. I dumped it in the back of the council wagon the next morning."

"Oh, well there goes my five hundred Euros."

"Tell me, Liz, how did you get into this Sally Ann lot? I would love to see you in the funny hat."

"No, I'm not with them. I saw the job advertised in the shop window. I walked in and had a rigorous interview, which lasted for about one minute, and I got the job. Sally Ann? Not me I was brought up as a catholic, you know the usual do what you like during the week and then into confession; confess to the priest say a couple of hail Mary's and the back out again, it was like sticking your clothes into the dry cleaner's. I soon gave up going to the Chapel. I was doing the 'business' in the 'Pool'; at the time, I was on heroin and weed and any other shit I could get. I was 'spaced out' most of the time. One night, one of my punters kicked shit out of me and left me for dead up an alley. Your lot the Bizzy's found me and I ended up in hospital. To cut a long story short, I was lying in my bed. I was totally fucked, Bob. An old Sally Ann officer, Major Mary, came and spoke to me. You know she was the first real person that had spoken to me in years. She didn't give a shit about my past. She held my hand, the first person in years to do that without wanting paid. When it was time for my discharge from the hospital, she was there waiting for me, second hand clothes all nicely cleaned and pressed, shoes the lot and fucking hand cream, Bob; nobody ever gave me hand cream in my life. She got me into one of their hostels and then a clinic. I'm clean now. I came out here to get away from all the shit, and then I found this job. I am sure it was meant to happen. I owe Major Mary and her Sally Ann crowd. Bob, they changed my life."

Tears slowly ran down her cheeks.

"Oh! Shit. Why am I telling you all this?"

I put my arm around her shoulder and gave her a cuddle. After another couple of drinks, we both went our separate ways. I only had two days of my holiday left; it was a charter job, so I did not have any option but to go.

The following morning, I was up bright and early and had a walk along the harbour and watching the rich of this world attending to their boats or at least their crews were.

I returned to my hotel had some breakfast and sat outside under the green canopy's reading about Allan Wicker's journeys and the interesting people he had met. It wasn't long before I heard the dulcet tones of Hugo. All the gusto seemed to have gone out of his voice. I looked up and there he was, a new bedraggled Hugo.

"Good morning, Bob. May I?"

He indicated with his outstretched hand to an empty chair next to me. I closed my book and looked up at him.

"Yes, certainly, how are you, sleep well?"

He pulled the chair from under the table and flopped into it. He stared at the book.

"No, I didn't. I had a hellish night I never slept a wink and you were the cause of it. No, I did not mean you were the cause, my life was going on as normal and then you come on the scene and start talking about all sorts of things and I lay tossing and turning all night. Why?"

"Try a new pillow, Hugo; there is no pillow as soft as a clear conscience and you know why, I want that phone number and that's all. Your grubby little secrets stay with me, and as you know, confession is good for the soul. Nobody else needs to know about your 'hobby'; do you understand?"

"Yes, I understand but I am so confused."

"What's causing the confusion?"

"Well, wouldn't you be confused? A guy arrives whom I don't even know and starts telling me about my past. I guess somehow you got hold of that tape. I never wanted anybody to know about it; my wife would kill me if she knew what I had done. If only she hadn't cleaned up and put them in that charity shop. I'll pay to have it back. Name your price."

"The phone number, that's all. The tape has been posted to my address in the UK. Once I have her number, the matter ends, but if I find out you have harmed that girl in any way, I will come back and kick shit out of you on behalf of her friend."

"I'm sorry she was never supposed to know the camera was there. I have the number here. It's in this diary she left behind when she ran off."

He then reached into the patch pocket of his trousers and produced a little floral diary. He handed it to me.

"Nobody knows I have it. The girl's name and phone number is in the back under contacts. It is the second one down, Tetyana."

I looked at the page and confirmed it; her name was followed by a London phone number. I put it in my pocket and stood up. Hugo took the hint and stood up too reaching out with his dead fish hand to shake mine. I kept my hand behind my back.

"Hope you don't mind if I don't shake hands just in case that was the one used in the shower with you, chum."

He ignored my comment.

"I hope this matter is now finished, Bob."

"Absolutely, old boy."

I looked at him as he shuffled away.

"Oh, sorry Hugo. Just one thing, why did you keep her diary?"

He stopped turned around and looked at me. He looked ashen.

"She went away without it. I found it under her bed. She must have dropped it."

He slowly walked off his head bowed.

I sat down, took a big sigh and thought, *What an arsehole.*

I spent most of the day reading through the diary. Most of the entries were in foreign language, presumably Ukrainian. There were a number that appeared to be UK telephone numbers.

My last night after my evening meal was spent in the El Casinet bar and as usual, Liz arrived and joined me.

"Well, Bob, home tomorrow, is it back to work?"

"No, I'm more or less retired now. I'm living on the Commissioners' pension now. I do a little bit of private work which pays for the odd holidays."

We talked well into the early hours of the morning and eventually went our separate ways. I was sorry to leave her. There was nothing in it. I just felt I had found a new friend. We exchanged addresses and telephone numbers. It's a strange thing policemen frequently develop friendships with people who have had a rough deal in life.

The morning came around all too soon and I boarded the coach and headed off to Palma Airport and eventually to Gatwick and then to my home in Berkshire and the usual heap of mail behind the front door.

It was like light years away from Puerto Pollenca and Hugo, or was it?

Chapter 6
The Diary

I walked to Wokingham, my nearest town and into the local coffee shop, ordered a coffee and sat down to read the morning papers.

"I see the traveller has returned; did you have a good time?" It was Sue, one of the waitresses.

"Yeah, just the usual, ate too much and lounged around."

"Only eating?"

"Well, I had the occasional glass of wine with my dinner; it is the local custom."

"Bob, I know you, was that one glass or one glass bottle?"

"Sue, girl, you know me too well."

"Bob, you need a good woman to keep you under control." She laughed and walked away from the table.

"Sue, before you go, is that little European bird working today?"

"She is not a bird nor little; she is a fine young girl and much too young for you. She is at college this morning doing her English course. She is in at one o'clock, why?"

"She's Russian or from around that way, isn't she?"

Sue looked at me with her eyes screwed up and her nose and mouth to one side.

"What you after, you dirty old git? She is a nice person and her name is Elensa."

"Sue, I am not old, just of advanced years. I am doing a little job and I would like to see if she could translate some entries in a diary for me. That's all!"

I finished my coffee and walked to the local hairdressers for a well-needed haircut. Later that afternoon, I returned to the coffee shop with a photocopied printout of the diary. Elensa was preparing Cappuccino's at the coffee machine. She looked over and smiled, as soon as the noise of the machine ceased she started to speak. Her luminescent smile appeared to light up the room. She was beautiful. Not a sex bomb; if anything, she oozed style and grace.

"Sue tells me you have been looking for me."

I was just about to say, 'yes, all my life' but thought better of it.

"Yes, I have a diary which I think is written in Ukrainian and I was hoping you might be able to give me an idea what it says, is that possible?"

"I'm Latvian, but I may be able to help. When do you want me to do it?"

"When you get a chance, I will pay you for your work."

She looked at me, smiled and tilted her head to one side.

"Don't be silly, Sue told me you are a detective. This is going to be exciting, like James Bond?"

"Well, more like Brooke Bond."

"Who is, how you say Brookey?"

I looked at her; she looked so innocent and yet exuding mystique.

"I have a copy with me perhaps you can take it with you and have a look at it in your spare time. I will give you my telephone number and perhaps you can give me a ring when you have had a chance to look at it." I started to walk out of the shop.

"Don't you want your coffee?"

I looked back over my shoulder. She had come from behind the counter holding a cup of coffee. I looked at her large blue eyes. What mysteries were locked away behind them? I took the coffee and sat at a table.

"Oh! I'm sorry I did not pay you."

"Have this one on the house; my boss has gone home."

I finished my coffee and left.

The following morning, my telephone rang.

"Hello, Mr Bob Bond, it's Elensa."

I knew right away I could not mistake her dulcet tones.

"I have looked at her diary. I suppose you understood it was a girl's. I think we should meet. It is very interesting; she did not like Mr H."

"When can I meet you?"

"I am not working tomorrow; perhaps I can see you then, Mr Bob."

"Okay, give me your address and I will pick you up and we can go for a meal."

"That would be very good."

"I will pick you up at about eight o'clock."

"That is a good time. I think you will find it interesting."

"Eight o'clock it is; see you then."

The line went dead. 'I think you will find it interesting'. Now, did she mean the contents of the diary? I put the phone down and stared at the handset. After a couple of minutes, I dialled a local number; the phone was answered.

"Rossini's Restaurant."

"Good evening, Tony, Bob MacInally here."

"Hello, Bob, what can I do for you?"

"Can I have a table for two tomorrow night; about eight thirty?"

"For you, my friend, no problem. One table for two reserved for eight thirty tomorrow night. Is she a looker?"

I laughed, it was always the same question; perhaps it was something in the Italian blood.

I met Elensa at her flat in the middle of Wokingham. She looked a million dollars. Long blonde hair hanging loosely over her shoulders, her blue eyes enhanced by the light blue eye shadow she was wearing. She looked at me in a questioning manner.

"Am I okay dressed like this? I was not sure what to wear."

She was wearing a white blouse and a black figure hugging pencil skirt, which was about knee length. Her high heel shoes brought her to about two inches beneath my height.

I swallowed hard and exaggerated a gulp.

"Yes, yes, you look first class. You look so different from the coffee shop."

"Different, what do you mean different?"

"Like a model." And with that, she punched me on my arm.

"A model? Come on, let's go."

We arrived at Rossini's' and were shown to our table by Tony. Once seated, Elensa produced the copies of the diary from her handbag.

"I can understand most of it. Some of the words I do not understand. Her name is Nadya; she has a good friend called Tetyana from Nadya's town. Tetyana visited her and stayed with her at a mister and misses, I think the name is Farter Brown."

I started to laugh.

"What did I say wrong?"

"Absolutely nothing. You got it perfectly correct. I will explain to you later, go on."

She smiled at me and carried on talking.

"Tetyana stayed with her and her family in February nineteen ninety-three. She writes she was happy to be with her friend who she had gone to school with and wished she could go with her friend who was going to go sailing. Tetyana had been asked to work on a boat with some people they had met in Palma. They were very rich people and were staying in an expensive hotel. She seems a happy person. Her birthday is on November 2. She will be going home to see her family for one week at that time."

Our meal arrived and we stopped talking about the diary. Elensa then started to ask me about my past. Was I married? Did I have any children? Had I a special lady?

I discovered she was thirty-seven, never been married, no children. She had been living with an Italian guy for two years, but he would not commit himself to any long-term thing. There was a young guy sniffing around, but he was too young for her. Was I in with a chance? I thought to myself.

"So you have no boyfriend?" I asked quizzically.

"No, but I have hundreds in queue. Why do you ask?" She smiled and tilted her head.

"You enjoying the meal?" I asked.

She smiled and shook her head as if to say crazy man and picked up the paperwork.

"Many telephone numbers are in the diary. I think most are from her country and some are from this country. She writes April, I think day four, and she put in her diary Mister Hugo is bad man. Why he have camera to do these things. Then she writes, bad, bad, he very bad man. Should I tell wife and then ????????? She puts all these things, what you call them? Questions. Yes."

She handed me the paper. I looked at it. It was, as she said question marks. I handed the paper back to her.

"Yes, these are question marks. You have done very well."

Tony topped up the wine glasses and gave me a wink.

Elensa raised her glass and said, "IKI."

I looked at her as I raised my glass and said, "CHEERS."

She touched her glass on mine and said, "You say Latvian, IKI," and with that, the glasses chinked.

"Bob, I think something not very nice happened to your friend. She went to the Catholic Church in the village and prayed that Mister H would be forgiven.

She then says she goes to bar and a nice lady called Liz who helped. She thinks lady is in an army."

I interrupted.

"No, she works in a shop which is run by The Salvation Army, a church outfit they wear uniforms, not bang, bang army: they help people, they helped Liz."

"Oh. I know in my country they are called Pestisanas Armija. Yes, I know now. Liz helped Nadya Not bang, bang army." We both laughed and went back to the translations.

"She writes many times she cries to sleep. She puts in diary I will go to London and live with Tetyana and then go on boat. On back pages, she has written words like cleaners, pharmacy and all words like that you know for supermarket. Oh yes and on one page in pencil, she writes, CROESUS. I am sorry that is all I do."

"Elensa, that is terrific; you have done a great job. I really want to try and find this girl."

"Is she your girlfriend?"

"No, I have never met her. Well, it is a very long story and I do not want to bore you with it."

Tony arrived at the table with a bottle of Limoncello and two ice-coated glasses.

"With the compliments of the house." He then walked off.

I started to relay the story to Elensa and after a few more glasses of the Italian liquor, I settled the bill and we left the restaurant. We slowly walked towards her flat. When we reached the entrance to her block, we stopped at the bottom of the staircase. I said my 'good nights'. She kissed me on my cheek and ran up the stairs as I stood and watched her. At the top of the stairs, she turned around and blew me a kiss from the palm of her hand. Her hand then changed as if holding a telephone and she mouthed, "Call me." And then giggled.

I walked home. It had been a good night. I felt I knew a lot more of Nadya but not enough of Elensa.

Chapter 7
Let's Try the Phone Numbers

The following morning, I was up at the crack of dawn and downstairs to put the kettle on. As I waited for it to boil, I found myself looking through the diary again. I started to compile a list of all the telephone numbers. There was about twenty for Latvia and only three for the London area.

I had some breakfast and then started phoning the numbers. One was discontinued another was unanswered. The third was a Park Lane Hotel in London. It was time to call in a favour. I telephoned the hotel and spoke to the chief security officer.

"Hello, shag nasty; how you doing?"

"Well, if it isn't Bob MacInally. How you doing, you old bugger?"

"Yeah, okay, Barry, do you fancy a little drink after you finish?"

"Sounds good to me, say five-thirty in the Running Footman in Charles Street. By the way, what are you after, Bob?"

"Barry, can't an old friend invite you for a drink without wanting something?"

"In your case no, I'll see you in the boozer at five-thirty, mate."

Barry was a first-class guy. I took him under my wing when he joined the Regional Crime Squad. A first-class copper but was always too active to study for promotion within the police.

He was waiting at the bar when I arrived, a pint of bitter waiting for me.

"Nice to see you, you old bugger." And with that, he gave me a hug and slapped me on the back.

"Been to Disneyland recently?"

"Piss off, one look at Donald Duck was enough for me."

Barry had been with me when I was shot. He travelled in the ambulance with me. Both he and his wife, Gloria, visited me every day I was in hospital.

"How's Gloria?"

"She's fine, got her own kiddies clothes shop in Chelsea and keeping me in the manner I was made for."

We got another couple of beers in and walked over to a table in the corner.

"What can I do for you, Bob?"

I explained the whole saga to him and then handed the Nadya letter written on his hotel's notepaper. He took it from me and studied it.

"Are the old bill involved in this?" I shook my head.

"Well as you, a 'crack detective' worked out it is from our hotel, then again the hotel name and address at the top may have given you a clue. But I bet you didn't know it is from one of our top suites, so the lady if she was staying there has got a few 'bob' or she had a rich punter. I suppose you want me to look at the hotel records to see who she was with?"

"That would be helpful and if there is anything else, I would be very grateful."

"How grateful?"

"Another pint?"

"Yeah, go on, big spender."

We passed the evening sorting out the world and all the dick heads that are running it.

At about eight o'clock, we went our separate ways. Barry promised me a phone call as soon as he had some news.

The following morning, I telephoned a contact that seemed to be able to get into the most confidential records. I was introduced to them by an ex-government spook. I explained that I wanted the subscribers to two telephone numbers and a breakdown of the numbers dialled. He took all the details and I gave him the number of a safe fax machine in a local print shop.

I sat back and waited. There was nothing I could do in the meantime. There was nothing else for it; the washing from the holiday had to be done. This living on your own is no good. Over the last thirty years or so, I had lived with a couple of women. They were not long-term things; one lasted six months. She told me we were not compatible; I think that was the word she used when she told me 'to piss off' and threw a black rubbish bag with all my worldly goods in it at me. She had a lovely body, but then that's not everything, or was it?

Oh well nothing else for it, get the ironing board out. Saying that reminds me of Noreen, pretty face body like an ironing board; mind you she did have a few quid. Top position in a large company, nice person but could not get enough sex.

I was the thinnest I had ever been. My mates at work thought I was ill. I had lost three stone and my eyes were like piss holes in the snow. She came in from work one night and told me she was moving out and going to move in with Sebastian in Chelsea. "We have been having an affair for six months." I was lost for words. She came down the stairs, cases packed and there was Sebastian sitting outside in his top of the Range Rover. Despite her protests, I carried her cases down to the car. Sebastian was on his telephone and blowing cigar smoke out of the open window. He nodded to me to put the cases in the rear of the car. I put them in as Noreen looked on 'no hard feelings, Bob?' I looked at her as she closed the tailgate.

"Don't be silly, darling."

I walked around to Sebastian he looked down his nose and smiled. "Thank-you, Bob."

I stared at him, "Are you the dirty bastard that gave me the pox?"

"What?"

At that point, Noreen was climbing into the car and bent over to kiss Sebastian on the cheek. He sharply pulled his face away from her mouth. I walked away scratching my nuts!

I often wonder how the journey back to Chelsea went.

My daydreaming ended as the phone rang.

"Hi Bob, Barry here, I've got quite a bit for you. Are you free tonight about six at the same boozer?"

"No problems. I'll see you there, cheers."

"Quite a bit?" Roll on six o'clock.

Chapter 8
It's a Start

I was half an hour early arriving at the pub. I sat in the corner reading the Evening Standard and sipping a pint. Right on time, Barry arrived. I folded my newspaper and walked over to the bar. The pub was filling up with office workers on the way home.

"Let's move on, Bob. There are a lot of our people in here tonight, some sort of leaving do."

We left the pub and walked towards Shepherd Market.

"Fancy a bite to eat, Barry?"

"I wouldn't say no. I spend all day working in hotels and walk out hungry, people don't believe it."

"Okay let's go to Da Corradi in the market. It's down to me."

"Fine by me; I've got some stuff you may be interested in. It would appear she and another girl booked in with some high rolling Arabs. They all gave the correct names, your lady and the other bird was booked in; they took three suites all booked through an agency. I looked at our occurrence book for the time they stayed. There was some sort of allegations of an indecent assault made by one of six Eastern European females who had been brought in for a party. Security were called and as my man was dealing with it, and about to call the police, a little Russian guy arrived and the allegation was withdrawn and that was the end of the matter. The Russian guy apparently had arranged the visit. I don't have his details. The bill for their stay was somewhere in the region of twenty-eight grand. I've got you a print out of the bills and all the phone numbers dialled from the rooms. They paid by credit card. I've got the details of that, the silly sods left their card behind reception. They discovered their loss when they got to Heathrow. The card came to me in the security office and I put it in my safe. Two days later, they sent a fax authorising a woman to collect it. I returned it personally to her. A tasty Eastern European bird aged about twenty years, gave her address as somewhere down in Chelsea. She had identification with her but no passport, said someone was holding it for her. I copied the lot and it's in the envelope. Don't open it here. I'm in the shit if the hotel discovers I've given it out to anyone."

We finished our meal and we went our separate ways. As soon as I got indoors, I was like a kid on Christmas morning. I searched through all the paper work until I found out who had collected that credit card, it didn't take long there it was in black and white.

COLLECTED BY: TETYANA PETROWSKI with an address in Sydney Street Chelsea London.

I read through the paper work into the early hours of the morning. What was I getting myself into? The following morning, I had all the information copied and I destroyed all of Barry's originals and any fingerprints, which may have been on them. I was now starting off with clean sheets.

I drove down to Chelsea and found the address it was a block of flats. I looked at the listing of names on the entry system. Flat 6, the one given by Tetyana Petrowski, had no name shown. I rang the bell. There was no reply. I kept the flat under observation for a few hours; apart from a few elderly people going in and out, there was no trace of 'my lady'. After having sat around for six hours, I walked down the road for a take away meal. I sat in the car eating 'supper'. After I had eaten as much as I could stomach, I walked back to the flats; I pressed the button for Flat 6. There was no answer but as I was about to walk away, a female voice answered.

"Hello." She had a very strong foreign accent.

I pressed the button again.

"Tetyana?"

"No, who is that?" She sounded drunk or suffering from a large hang over.

"My name is Bob. I'm a friend of Tetyana. I have message for her." She mumbled something and then I heard the door lock click and the heavy mahogany door opened. I walked into a beautifully furnished hallway. I slowly entered and walked past a hall table with an expensive bronze sculpture of what appeared to be a Roman Centurion. There were three doors to flats on the ground floor. I walked up the deep piled stair carpet held in place with highly polished stair rods. The balustrade on my left was a work of art. I reached the second landing door number six was ajar.

"Hello, Tetyana?" I waited; there was no reply.

"Tetyana."

No reply. I pushed the door. It opened about twelve inches and then it jammed. I shouted her name again. There was a muffled sound from behind the door. I squeezed in through the gap. Lying on the floor was a beautiful woman aged about twenty years. Her silk dressing gown had fallen open revealing her in all her glory. I soon found out she was breathing. There was no smell of alcohol. I attempted to revive her; I then became aware of someone looking down at me. It was an elderly couple.

"Don't move. We have called the police. What have you done to her?"

"Nothing, have you called an ambulance?"

"The police said they would call an ambulance, and if you think of running, I have locked the front so you are not getting out of here." I looked at the poor old soul who was doing her best. I just could not help thinking she had been reading too many Miss Marple books.

"Madame, I have done nothing, now go downstairs and let the emergency services in."

I indicated to the male. "You get a blanket for her." In the meantime, I was covering her with my jacket and trying to give what assistance I could. I heard the front door opening and could hear the commotion as the police and ambulance people arrived accompanied by the voice of the lady telling them that her husband had detained the 'culprit'.

I looked up from where I was kneeling; an ambulance man was standing outside the door his head peering around towards me.

"You'll have to squeeze through, mate. I haven't moved her."

I stood up and allowed the two ambulance men in. As I did so, I noticed a plastic medicine bottle lying on a coffee table. The lid was off and a couple of tablets were lying next to it. I picked it up; it had contained Paracetamol tablets. The label on the bottle was from a chemist shop on the Kings Road in Chelsea. A bottle of whiskey together with a glass sat next to the tablets. I picked the glass up and sniffed it. It had not been used. I looked over to the ambulance men.

"It looks as if she may have taken some tablets; there is an empty Paracetamol bottle here."

"Yeah, we thought so. My mate's gone for a stretcher and we will get her off to hospital and get her pumped out, are you a relative?"

Before I could answer, the other ambulance man arrived with a stretcher chair and they gently lifted her on to it. I opened the door. Two uniformed cops were standing on the landing. The younger of the two was interviewing the elderly couple and making notes.

"We are taking her to St Thomas; we don't have any particulars for her." The police officer looked up. "We will see you over there, cheers mate."

"That's him, he was bending over her naked body, and I saw him."

I was getting a little pissed off by 'Miss Marple'. She was all set to have me hanged.

As the ambulance men reached the half landing, a man who introduced himself as the porter said, "What's going off governor?"

The elder of the two police officers looked at the porter and me; he let out a sigh.

"Come on, let's get into the flat and sort this out."

We walked in and stood around.

"Now you are the caretaker, sir? Let me get your details first."

"Full name?"

"George Winston Dixon."

"When were you born, George?"

"May 28 1962."

"And where was that?"

"London Hospital, Mile End Road, I'm a good London boy."

"What height are you George, five feet eight or nine?"

"I'm about five feet nine, difficult to tell these days left a leg in the Falklands."

"What was that George, the Army?"

"Yeah, the 'Paras', happy days."

"Thanks and you, sir, your full name please."

"Robert William Wallace MacInally."

"And where were you born, Robert?"

"Glasgow, nineteen forty-five, six feet one inch."

"That was quick, Robert. Know the system, do we?"

"A bit."

He then nodded to the younger P.C. who then walked out on to the landing. I could hear him on his radio checking us out with the Police National Computer. He then walked back into the room his radio burst into life 'three twenty-one can you talk?' he then walked out of the room. I could hear he was on the radio but could not make out what he was saying but I had a good idea.

"Do you 'live in', Mr Dixon?"

"Yeah, basement flat, I'll be in all night."

"Okay, we will pop down and see you shortly." And with that, George left the flat.

"Right, Robert, a quick word in your ear."

"Call me Bob; everybody does."

"Okay, Bob, what exactly is your business in this flat and who is the young lady, and most of all, how did you get in to a locked flat?"

I started to explain. "I met a couple in Spain. Nadya had written to them and they wanted me to speak to Tetyana to try and find her." The more I spoke, the more it sounded so implausible.

"Now, Bob, from the beginning. This family in Majorca. What is their address and phone number?"

"I don't know their exact address or phone number."

"Bob, turn out your pockets. Have you got anything on you, you shouldn't have?"

I turned out my pockets and put the contents on the coffee table. The younger of the two searched my wallet and took out one of my old business cards and handed it to the other cop. He read it out loud.

"Robert W. W. MacInally GM, Private Investigator, from Wokingham in Berkshire. Just how did you get into these flats and this one in particular?"

"The young lady pressed the intercom. I came up the stairs, her door was ajar. I called her name. She didn't answer. I pushed the door and squeezed in."

"What is her name, Bob?"

"I don't know."

"And you called out her name?"

"Not her name, Tetyana's."

"Robert MacInally, I am arresting you on suspicion of breaking into this flat. You do not have to say anything but it may harm your defence if you do not mention when questioned something which you later rely on in court. Anything you do say may be given in evidence."

I held out my hands. The handcuffs were snapped on. The cop smiled; a knowing smile as I held my hands out.

"Done this before, have we, Bob?" I smiled back.

"A few times but usually the other way around."

"Prefer your hands behind your back?"

"Something like that."

I was ceremoniously put in the police car and taken to Chelsea Police Station.

On arrival, I was taken into the custody suite and the arresting officer relayed to the custody sergeant (who looked as if he had just come out of school) what had happened.

"I'm satisfied with what the officer has told me. You will be detained in this police station whilst the officers make further enquiries."

I found myself in cell three sitting on the bed. Nothing else for it but to wait for the interview, which would happen soon. Oh shit! I've got Barry's hotel documents in the car. If the 'old bill' finds them, questions will be asked and Barry could lose his job.

An hour or so passed and the cell door opened.

"Here you are, sir, (he handed my belt, tie and shoes from outside the cell.) CID wants a word with you." As I walked down the corridor towards the interview a room, I felt a slap on my back.

"What you doing here, shag nasty?"

I looked around. It was a cop I had worked with when I was stationed in the East End of London.

"Pussy Johnson, where have you been hiding for all these years?"

"I've been on attachment to the Home Office for a few years and then they found me out and I ended up here. The last I heard of you was when you went out on a pension after you were shot in that South London caper. What are you doing here?"

"Nicked for giving first aid to some bird."

The officer escorting me looked on in disbelief.

"And that was a very serious assault; it will cost the Commissioner a few quid."

"Give me a shout when you're finished whatever you're up to and we will have a beer. You always did play it close to your chest."

Pussy walked off and I was ushered into the interview room where my arresting officer was waiting along with a female officer in plain clothes. My escorting officer bent down to the female officer and whispered in her ear. She stood up and both of them walked out of the room. After a few minutes, the female officer returned, pulled up a chair and sat facing me.

"I am Detective Sergeant Margaret Cassidy; you have already met Sergeant Dean. This interview will be recorded and I must remind you, you are still under caution. However, before we start, I understand you have had dealings with Chief Inspector Johnson and I further understand you are making an allegation of assault against him. Is that correct?"

"Pussy, a Chief Inspector, you're having a laugh."

"No, Mister MacInally. I am not having a laugh as you put it. Do you wish to continue with this complaint?"

"Piss off. I would no more fly in the air than make a complaint against Derek and anyway, what's all this crap about a complaint?"

"You were overheard to say you would meet him for a drink after. Was that a suggestion of some form of a gratuity for a favour you are expecting over this case?"

"What bloody case, you lady have nothing on me. Now I am saying nothing until you switch the bloody tape on." She stared at me and waited for me to react. The other officer leant back his hands clasped behind his head. She continued staring as she leant forward and pressed the record button. Slowly and deliberately, she cautioned me again, stated her and the other officer's name followed by mine.

"Mr MacInally, you were found in Flat Six Phoenix buildings this afternoon. What was the nature of your business at the flat?"

"Before I answer that question, I would like to make a statement for the benefit of the tape. Before this tape was switched on, Detective Sergeant Brooks alleged that I was making an allegation of assault against Chief Inspector Derek Johnson at this police station. This is completely untrue. She further suggests that there is something corrupt taking place between us. Yes, Derek Johnson did hit me a couple of times but that was when we were training for the Lafone cup and in case Ms Cassidy is not aware, that is the cup awarded in the Metropolitan Police Boxing Championship. Two hits from him and I was knackered and I was counted out. We became close friends and I attended his daughter's wedding and yes we have been out and got pissed on many occasions much to the annoyance of his wife Claire who frequently let me kip in their spare room."

"So are you telling me you are a former police officer?"

"No, I am not telling you anything. I think you have detected that yourself and before you even suggest it, I am not looking for any favours. Now can we get on with this enquiry and may I suggest you start at St Thomas' Hospital and see if that kid has come around and she may well confirm my story."

She reached over towards the tape recorder and whilst staring at me, spat out, "Interview terminated at six thirty." She then stamped out of the room, looked over her shoulder and spoke to the other officer.

"Stay with him."

We sat in silence, with me staring at the ceiling and the uniformed officer doodling on a notepad. Eventually, the officer broke the silence.

"So you were in the job, governor?"

"Yeah, I'm out on an ill health pension. I tried to get them to let me stay but they would not have it."

"So what did you finish up as?"

"DS on a crime squad."

"What happened then, gov?"

"An arsehole shot me at the scene of a blag."

"Is that where the George Cross came from?"

"Yep, seems like a long time ago when I sit here now listening to that so-called DS. I get the impression she could not detect a pickle onion in a fruit salad."

"Don't quote me but she's hated in the nick, hates Mr Johnson, always trying to drop him in the shit." He had just finished talking when the interview room door burst open and in walked Brooks considerably more subdued than when she had left. She placed an A4 folder on the desk. She looked straight at me.

"I have spoken to the Pension Department and they tell me you retired on an ill health pension."

I interrupted her.

"What the hell has that got to do with me being banged up here for being a suspect in a non-existent screwing of the flat and if you had your way, you would be trying to make out I had also screwed the kid in the flat."

"I can only go on what evidence is put in front of me."

"There was fuck all evidence. Now would you please tell me what is going on as far as my detention here is concerned? I suppose you are aware how much the Commissioner pays out for unlawful detention of the public purse and that's not going to do your future promotion much good."

"Mr MacInally, the young lady has gained consciousness and she confirms that a Tetyana does live at the flat and as far as she can remember, someone did ring the entry system and asked for Tetyana. You will be released from this station after we have completed some formalities. Miss Domitrevich will be kept in the hospital overnight. You are free to go."

She stood up jerked her head to one side indicating to the uniform cop to get me out of the building. We walked to the front door. As I was leaving, he turned around and we shook hands.

"I'm John Miller, just call me 'Dusty'; everyone does. Nice to have met you. By the way, I'm going over to Saint Thomas. If you hold on, I'll give you a lift over and I will introduce you to Vesta. After all you did save her life."

I accepted the lift.

"You know, Bob, Sergeant Brooks is not that bad. It's just that she does not like Chief Inspector Johnson one little bit. I saw her coming out of his office a few weeks back. I don't know what it was all about but she was raging so much so she bumped into me as she mumbled 'I'll have that bent bastard one day'. I jokingly said sorry meaning sorry for bumping in to her. She took my arm, looked at me and said no it was my fault. She smiled and said I thought you had heard what I said. I shrugged my shoulders and laughed and walked down the corridor putting my hands over my ears and saying. Speak no evil, hear no evil, see no evil. You know, Bob, she's a good cop but Johnson hates her guts. I think she has something on him. You know what the job's like."

Within about thirty minutes, we were walking into the hospital ward. A nurse took us to the bed where Vesta was sitting up resting against some pillows. Dusty looked at the newspaper next to her bed.

"Learning about all the things that are happening in Britain?"

"I only read a little my English is not very good."

She looked quizzically and yet with an air of shyness. Dusty spoke, "This is Bob who helped you, he is a friend of. Sorry, Bob, I cannot remember the girl's name."

"Tetyana." Vesta pushed herself off the pillows.

"You are a friend of Tetyana. She is with, maybe a man; his name is Walter; who is Walter Bob? I too am looking for Tetyana."

"Vesta, tomorrow I will come and see you and we can talk about it okay?"

"The doctor comes at eleven in the morning and then I think I go home."

"Okay, Vesta, I will come and see you tomorrow."

Chapter 9
Let's Find Walter

The following day, I visited the ward and was told it would be another hour before the doctor would be doing his rounds. I walked down to the restaurant and sat down with my coffee and a newspaper. It seemed every nationality from around the world was here to get free medical treatment; well not free, I and others like me have been paying for it for years. Now don't get bitter, Bob, they are all God's children. I could hear the voice of the hospital Chaplin from years before. After about an hour, I walked back to the ward and spoke to the senior nurse on duty.

"Good morning. Is it all right to go and see Miss Domitrevich?"

"Oh dear, you have just missed her. Her uncle the Russian man brought her clothes in and they have just left."

I ran to the lifts and entered, reached the ground floor after being messed about by people who could not make up their minds as to which floor they wanted and held the doors open whilst they decided. I walked into the foyer and standing at the public phones was Vesta. She was standing next to a man aged about fifty years. He was heavy built with grey hair swept back with the front pulled forward in a Toni Curtis style. As I walked towards Vesta, she slowly shook her head from side to side; she looked terrified. The man she was with was on the telephone. I walked over to an unattended phone close to him; I dialled my home number and listened to my answer machine. The man was talking in what appeared to be Russian. Whilst listening to the caller on the other end of the line, he turned to Vesta and started to stroke her cheek with the back of his hand. It was obvious that she was not enjoying it. She was like a frightened pup. As she slowly moved her face away, he took her face between his thumb and forefinger and turned her head towards him and put the phone to her ear. She said one word and then listened; she then said another one, maybe two words and pulled her head away. Her 'uncle' sniggered and then silently laughed as he replaced the handset. Taking hold of her hand, they both walked to the front exit and hailed a passing cab; both got in it made a 'U' turn towards Lambeth Bridge. I ran down the stairs to jump into a cab and follow them; as usual that only happens in the movies, no empty cabs were passing. By the time I reached my car and drove off, they had well gone. I fought my way through the London traffic and parked up near Phoenix Buildings and watched the entrance to the flats. After about one hour, I saw the curtains in flat six being moved slightly and a figure looked out from behind the curtain. A taxi pulled up and double-parked. After a few minutes, a man ran down the outside steps, climbed into the back of the cab and the cab drove off. It was the man from the hospital. I followed the cab to Bayswater Road where it stopped outside Kensington Palace Gardens. The man got out and paid the driver. I picked up my Nikon camera and ran off six or seven frames as he walked into the Palace Gardens past the security people. I jumped out of my car and ran up to the wrought iron gates in time to see 'my man' turn left into the entrance of the Russian Embassy. Returning to my car, I was just in time to stop a Traffic Warden issuing a ticket, boy was I eating large portions of 'humble pie' as I spoke to her. Getting into my car and fastening my seat belt, I looked out at her and she was signalling 'get moving'. I blew her a kiss and she mouthed 'bollocks'. I burst out laughing followed by her. She waved and walked off. A traffic warden with a sense of humour; things can only get better. Who the hell is the guy at the Embassy? Why was he treating Vesta in the manner he was at the hospital and why did she not wish me to speak to her? She knew I was coming to collect her why didn't she wait for me? Too many unanswered questions and most of all; what was I getting into?

Let's go and meet Vesta.

As usual, parking spaces around Chelsea were as scarce as rocking horse shit. Eventually after driving around for ages, I found a parking space close to Vesta's flat. I waited for any signs of movement; after about an hour I took the bull by the horns and walked over to the entrance to the flats and pressed the bell for Flat 6. I waited for anther few minutes and tried again the entry system burst in to life, a woman answered in a foreign language.

"Vesta?"

"Who is it, what you want?"

"Vesta, it's Bob from the hospital. Are you okay?"

"You go and stand in street so I see you."

I walked into the street and looked up once again. The curtain opened and I could see Vesta. She waved down and beckoned me to come up. As I reached the bottom of the steps, the entry buzzer was sounding. I pushed the door. It opened and I walked into the hallway and up the staircase all too familiar to me now. Vesta was standing at the open door. She put her finger over her mouth and with her other hand, gestured to me to come in quickly; as I entered the hallway, she immediately closed and locked the door behind me.

"I am sorry I must keep the door closed. I am frightened, so many bad things."

"Vesta I am Bob; I am trying to find Tetyana. Don't worry I will not harm you."

"Why do you want Tetyana?"

"She is a friend of Nadya who was working in Mallorca."

"I have heard that name but I do not know her; she is supposed to be staying at Walter's house. Maybe they are both with Walter?"

"Vesta, who told you these things?"

"The Russians."

"Who are the Russians; what have they got to do with it?"

She looked at me totally terrified. "I am sorry I say too much. They must not find you here or you are in big trouble and I also go to stay at Walter place. Give me your telephone number and I will telephone tomorrow and we go for coffee with Peter. Yes?"

"Yes, but who is Peter?"

"Peter Jones, the big department, Sloane Square; now you must go quickly, okay?"

"Okay?"

With that, I left the flat and returned to my car.

There were so many things to think over and try to work out; most of all who the hell is Walter? Was he the person who went to the Russian embassy, was he Walter?

I drove along the M4 Motorway and by the time I reached the sign for Wokingham, I still did not have any answers.

No sooner had I got indoors when my phone rang. It was the print shop in Wokingham.

"Hi, Bob, it's Michele; there are some faxes in for you."

"Okay. I'll pick them up first thing in the morning."

I lay back on my settee and started to watch the news on television. The day's events ran through my mind; I dozed off, and wakened with a start, it was the telephone. I managed to answer it before the voicemail kicked in.

"Bob MacInally."

"Hello, Bob, Vesta speaking."

"Oh hi, Vesta, is everything okay?"

"Yes, okay; can we meet tomorrow at ten o'clock in Peter Jones café. I may have to go away for a few days."

"Yeah, that is fine. I will see you then."

She rang off. What would tomorrow bring?

Chapter 10
I Am So Frightened

Vesta was already having a coffee when I arrived at the coffee shop. She had a bit more colour in her face from when I saw her last. Dressed in blue jeans, knee high brown leather boots, a black bomber jacket and a red roll neck sweater; her long hair hidden beneath a baseball cap.

"Good morning, Vesta."

She looked up startled and then suddenly relaxed when she saw me.

"Oh, Bob, I'm sorry I arrived early; I left the house early before any visitors arrived."

"Visitors, I'm sorry were you expecting people to your flat?"

"Yes, it's the Russians. They call at different times to make sure I am still living there."

"Vesta, I do not understand what is going on and by the sound of the very little I have heard, it will take some time to hear the full story. Have you got time to tell me today?"

"Yes, I am not going back to the flat until four o'clock. I have left a note in my flat. Perhaps we can go somewhere else and I will tell you the story and maybe you find Nadya and Tetyana, yes?"

We left the coffee shop and got into a cab.

"Villiers Street, Gordon's Wine Bar." The cab driver acknowledged my instructions with the accepted norm; a nod of the head and 'cheers Gov'.

We were soon at Villiers Street and made our way down Watergate Walk and into the oldest wine bar in London and possibly the world; it's history dates back to thirteen sixty-four with the most recent 'refurb' being in eighteen ninety. It is an ideal meeting place, the wood panelled walls are covered with historical newspapers telling stories of past world events. Bending our heads, we walked into the cave like area where no two chairs or tables were alike. I found a table in the candle lit area, Vesta sat down and I made my way to the bar, collected a bottle of Rivallan Tinto Rioja and two glasses. As I arrived back, Vesta was paring the wax that had dripped from the single candle stuck in the neck of an old wine bottle. I poured the wine and we raised our glasses touching them gently. Vesta's hand shook as she put the glass on the table.

"Bob, I am very frightened. I have got involved with some very bad Russian men. I am from Ukraine my family is good family. I was working in a small company in Kiev, I was in the office; they supplied air conditioning for people. One day in the newspaper, I see advert for photo models to work for advertising agency promoting Ukraine in London. I apply and they tell me I am very good, they take lots of pictures, not naughty you know. I have all my clothes on. They then do pictures of me in our national dress; you know the embroidered bluzah."

"Sorry what is a blasa?"

"Not blasa, a bluzah, you know like lady jumper but silk with buttons down front and little pockets here."

And with that, she opened her jacket and put her hands under her large perfectly shaped breasts.

"Ah! A blouse."

I tried not to stare too much.

"Yes, blouse, it is very pretty with lots of nice sewing, you know flowers and things."

She closed her jacket all too soon.

"After a few days, I went to a hotel in Kiev, you know our Capital. There were six other girls there and we all sat around a table. The lady and the man said we had all been chosen for the trip. We would stay in London in big hotel and then be taken to tourist places and have more pictures for tourist book. They would pay all expenses and we would get about eight hundred pounds for the two weeks. This was good for us."

"We arrived in London and people meet us with little bus. The man say, problem at London hotel we go to boss man's big house in country. We drive for one maybe two hours and arrive at big house in country. A lady comes to the big doors and says welcome to England; men take our cases and show us our rooms. We are told welcome party in one hour. I knocked on door of other Ukraine girls; we were all laughing and having fun as we went down the stairs. The lady was at bottom she says, 'follow me' and we all then go into big, big room. You know, like a palace; we have drinks, Champagne. Then we have little food. I had never been in such a place my head goes funny, not drunk funny very strange feeling.

I remember lady say come and I show you house. She takes my arm and I start to walk upstairs. I think I only drink a little and now I feel strange not drunk just strange. At top of stairs, she says this is very nice room; she says you like?"

The tears started to run down Vesta's cheeks. I took out my handkerchief and handed it to her. I was glad I had ironed it earlier. She wiped the tears from her face. I felt she did not have to tell me much more. I guessed what was coming next, or at least I thought I did.

"Bob, I was a good girl; I never been with a man, you understand?"

I nodded.

"She then led me into the room. Sitting in a big chair was a man smoking a big cigar. I remember the smell. He had a glass in the other hand. I think to myself, he is very big and fat and the same age as my father. The woman say Vesta darling, this is Ameer. He put his glass down and with his hand, he waves me over to chair. I am very weak. The lady helps me over. She says Ameer this is Vesta you like? He says, and I will never forget, I am Ameer the Ruler, the Prince. He pulled me onto his knee. I do not remember anything more. I waken in bed, the sun is shining, I have no clothes on, bites on my body you know he bites me all over I can't move. Bob, you understand I tell you I have never been with man, honest. I look over and see his cigar in tray, glass full he not drink. I sat on bed crying for my mother I look at floor, all my clothes on floor. My panties are all, how you say 'torn'."

I nodded; the anger was boiling inside me.

"Yes, torn." I could barely say the word. I was full of anger filled with compassion.

"The lady who took me to the room came in the next morning. She was laughing and asked me if I have good time. The lady she is pig lady."

She sobbed and tried to get her breath.

"Bob, one day I kill the bastard man, yes?"

"Not if I get there first."

She sipped her wine, her hands shaking as she did so.

"Have you ever seen him since?"

"No, I think they live in a house in the South of France."

"Vesta, I know these people do very bad things to keep girls under their control, what are they doing to you?"

"They know so many things about my family; they say they will hurt them or even kill. They were working with secret police, how you say KGB."

"Yes, KGB."

"When wall in Berlin comes down, they know many secrets of families."

"Tell me, Vesta, what happened after you stayed at the house?"

"The people there keep us for some days. They give us good food but all the time, they warn us to do what we are told or our families at home will be killed or the children would be taken away and held until, how you say, 'we behave ourselves'. They then bring very nice clothes and make us try them on; they were very good clothes better than I had ever had. The pig lady says that I was very lucky because the man who hurt me had picked me out from the pictures they had taken and I was the best. She said he was very pleased with me. I felt as if I was a cow or a dog for sale; like you know a; how you say, market.

"We were then taken to big hotels in the good clothes and then made to have sex with more Arab men. These Arab men are supposed to be good men, you know with their religion, they not drink alcohol or have sex with other woman. Ugh!"

Chapter 11
Let's Find Ameer

We left the wine bar and got a taxi back to Chelsea. I dropped Vesta off in Sloane Street. She promised to phone me the next day. I returned to Wokingham and collected my faxes from the printers. There were a number of addresses from the list of phone numbers I had given my contact. The one that stood out was for Robert Parker at Braithwaite Manor in Dummer in Berkshire just off the M3 Motorway. The telephone was registered to him. I searched the Electoral Register; there was nobody registered at the address, which in itself was rather strange. What was the connection with a manor house; there was nothing else for it I would have to take a trip down to Dummer.

Dummer Stores

I arrived in Dummer early the following morning; it was a beautiful morning with a slight mist rising off the fields. The rising sun was burning off the mist. Wearing my rambler's kit, a local map in its plastic wallet hanging around my neck and my 'happy wanderer' kit bag on my back. I set off leaving my car some two miles outside the village. I walked into the village passing the white painted Dummer Stores and the Post Office. On my left, its red painted telephone box with all its windows intact set a scene captured from bygone years. I continued past All Saints' Church. In this picture post card village, anyone asking directions to a particular house or property would be the talk of The Queen Inn, the village local pub. I walked into Dummer Down Lane and past Bible Fields; what a strange name for a road. As I continued down the lane, I could hear the sound of a car being driven fast along this single-track road. It came screeching around the bend. I dived into the hedgerow and fell onto the grass verge. The car, a large black Mercedes raced passed. I was dusting myself down when the obscenities I was mumbling under my breath were interrupted by a female voice. I looked up, a middle-aged woman dressed in a floral dress and wearing walking boots was standing at the five-bar gate; two Cocker Spaniel dogs were by her side, their tails waging furiously.

"I avoid the road since these damn Russians moved in. They have no respect for the locals; they think because they are stinking rich they own the village. Oh, sorry I'm Violet."

"Bob MacInally." I reached out and shook her hand; the dogs growled. I stepped back.

"Seb; Casper, sit!" The dogs immediately came to heel and sat down.

"Sorry about that, they tend to look after me. Are you okay?"

"Yes, I'm fine. I trust my mumbled swearing did not disturb you?"

"Not one bit, they have heard a lot more from me because of their driving. We thought we would be getting good neighbours when they bought the Manor."

"They are not short of money if they can afford to buy a Manor."

"My chum's husband owns the estate agents that sold Braithwaite. It went for somewhere in the three-million-pound region. It was a cash deal I believe it's a big estate, one of the biggest in the area, not as big as Major Ferguson's though."

"Major Ferguson?" I asked.

"Yes, you know his daughter, Sarah, who married Prince Andrew."

"Ah yes, Fergie, the one who appeared on the Sunday having her toe sucked by the bald geezer."

"We don't talk about that around these parts, at least not in public." She gave me a 'knowing smile'.

"You are not from the press, are you?"

"No, not me, on holiday just trying to get a bit of exercise. I am visiting family in Southampton. Have you lived here long?"

"Yes, my family have lived here for years. My father and his father before him were the estate manager at Braithwaite Manor. When Sir Walter, the original owner, died away back in the last century, his son inherited the estate, blew the money on wine, women and song and then wasted the rest. He in turn died and the estate went to some Aussie relatives. The trouble is the new occupants have no class. The caretaker had been there for years. He left, said there was all sorts of strange things going on; never did say what, although by the amount of rubbish they put out on a Tuesday night for collection they must go through some amount of Vodka."

"It looks as if the driver of the car may well have been on the Vodka in the manner he was driving, I'll keep out of his way and the Manor."

"Well, if you keep going in that direction, he will hit you on his return. The Manor is about one mile up the road on your right, safe journey and happy holidays." And with that, she walked into the field with her dogs that were now chasing a ball she had thrown.

"Bye."

What a nice woman, I didn't have to ask one question and yet she told me mostly everything I wanted to know; a good result.

I continued down the country lane when after about a mile, there it was Braithwaite Manor, or at least the entrance. Two large wrought iron gates with two cast sailing ships in full sail on each gate. On the right-hand pillar was what appeared to be an entry phone system. Walking further down the lane, I found a gap in the hedgerow. I looked about, there was nobody around; I jumped into the ditch and scrambled up the other side and through the gap and into an overgrown wooded area. Making my way through this, I eventually reached an open space with beautifully manicured lawns. I hid in the undergrowth and observed the view. To the front of the manor house was a lawn about the size of a football field, a paved area surrounding a large pond and a fountain cascading water over ornamental figures. Situated on top was another cast metal sailing ship similar to the ones on the gates; this one was made out of copper and had turned green over the years. I could imagine coach and horses pulling up outside in the good old days, today a Bentley and a Rolls Royce; both top of the range sat outside leaving space for at least another thirty cars. The house itself had at least twenty sash windows; to the front was a highly polished double door entrance. The doors were at the top of a flight of stairs. Six pillars supporting a balcony covered the entrance. From the amount of chimney-stacks, I could see I guessed there were at least twenty-five rooms. I took a few photographs of the property and as I was doing so, the Mercedes that I had seen earlier arrived. The driver, a little stocky guy about five feet six inches tall wearing a blue open necked polo shirt ill-fitting sports jacket and black trousers. He looked as if he had just walked out of a working men's club. The passenger got out, a tall bearlike man. I photographed them and left the area and made my way back across fields to my car. On my return to Wokingham, I put the film in for processing and collection the following morning.

I checked my answering machine. There was a message from Vesta.

'Hi Bob, it's Vesta. If you are free tomorrow, I would like to meet with you in the morning in market place at St James's Church in Piccadilly between eleven thirty and twelve o'clock. Lots of things are happening, Vesta.'

Chapter 12
Who Is in the Photos?

Dummer

The following morning, I walked into Wokingham and collected the prints from the photo shop and made my way by train to Waterloo station, and took a taxi to Lower St James Street and then strolled towards Piccadilly past the exclusive and expensive shops. Within a few minutes, I was in the market place in front of the church. Vesta was standing next to one of the many stalls she was examining some of the handmade crafts. She turned around and saw me.

"Hi, Bob. Thanks for coming. I hope you did not mind me phoning?"

"No, not at all. Let's walk over to the Regent Palace Hotel and have a coffee, okay."

"Yes, as long as the bad people are not in coffee place."

"No, the Regent Palace Hotel is not frequented by rich Arabs or Russians."

We walked through the front door of the hotel and made our way through the queues of guests waiting to check in; at Johnstone's café, we sat down at a corner table.

"Bob, some Russians came to the flat last night. They were very drunk and were talking something about going to a boat with six girls for Arab men. I heard them say they had the girls and they would do what they were told to do, not like the bitch Tetyana. Then one say is she still at Mr Stanley's house."

"Did they say where the house was?"

"I don't think they say, but the little bad dressed man who owns the flat took an old watch from his pocket and opened the lid and said something like 'Mr Stanley's says it is time to go'. He then put watch back in pocket; they all stood up and walked out laughing. My grandfather had a watch like it, it had a little chain like last night's watch, Grandfather's was a poor man's watch; not gold like the Stanley man's one."

"How many Russians were there?"

"Four; they were saying something about taking us on a boat. You understand they were talking very quickly and I did not understand everything. As they were leaving, the little one held my face between his fingers and squeezed very hard. He said, you be good girl."

I nodded and took my photographs out of the envelope. Vesta started crying.

"He said if I was naughty, I would go to stay with Tetyana at Mr Stanley's house."

I laid the pictures out on the table in front of Vesta.

"These are the pictures I took yesterday. Do you recognise any of the places or people?"

She started to sob as she pushed a picture of Braithwaite Manor towards me.

"This is the house where they took me when I arrived in your country, this is it."

She slowly pushed it to one side and looked at the pictures of the men.

"That one was at the house last night." She pointed to the big man in the picture.

"The little man he was there. He has the watch; I tell you he owns flat. He is man who came to hospital. I think he is boss man."

I started to put the pictures back in the envelope. Vesta looked at my hands as I collected them off the table.

"What is that one?"

"Which one?" She reached out and pointed.

"Oh, that is only one of the gates at the front of the house."

"May I see it?"

She reached out and I handed the picture to her. She studied it for some time and then slowly looked up.

"These ships on the gate, I have seen them before."

She kept studying the picture; I looked at her.

"Perhaps you saw them when you were at the house. There is a fountain at the front door and there is one there."

"No, no, I have seen it after the house, I know. It is on a key at the flat where you found me. It is a very old key and brown as if having been in water. The Russian calls it Stanley's key; can I borrow your pen?"

I handed her my pen and a piece of paper. She slowly drew an image of the key; it was about six inches long from the front to the rear of the shank. The working end was like an old-fashioned rim lock key. On the other end, she started to draw an ornamental ring, inside this she drew a sailing ship in full sail.

"I am sorry it is not very good picture, it looks like it a little."

"Vesta, where is that key now?"

"It is at the flat I think. He keeps it in a drawer in the little table."

"Is it at the house now?"

"I think so he only takes it out some days only for two, three hours and then he always bring it back and put it in the drawer. Why?"

"Could you bring it out of the house for five minutes today?"

"I could get it tonight after ten o'clock."

We got into a taxi and headed to Kings Road.

"Bob, do you think the key is for Mr Stanley's house and Tetyana?"

"It would appear to belong to a very old lock; I will be able to have better idea when I see it. I will be in your street at nine o'clock. When you can get out, I will follow you and if everything is okay just say 'Bob' as I pass you and I will stop in a doorway further down the road and then you can show me the key; if you are not happy just keep walking; okay?"

"Okay, I will do my best." She left the cab and walked off; I continued down Kings Road, paid the cabbie and then made my way to a local pet shop and bought a couple of pieces of Cuttlefish bone and then to the sweet shop and bought a tin of extra strong mints. I emptied the mints into my pocket. Further down the road, I found an old-fashioned hardware store. The elderly shop assistant dressed in a brown warehouse coat looked over the top of his half-moon spectacles.

"Yes, sir, what can I do for you?"

"I would like a couple of sheets of fine sandpaper and a flat file."

He turned around; opened a couple of drawers and brought out two sheets of sandpaper. Reaching over he opened another drawer looked in and mumbled.

"Looks like I've only got one flat bastard left, will that do?" He held up a ten-inch file.

I nodded he put the goods in a brown paper bag and I paid him and left the shop. I walked towards the Thames embankment and sat down on a bench overlooking the south side. I kept thinking what an old git swearing as he did, I wonder what his customers thought of him?

I opened the bag and took out the file; I could not believe my eyes, there on the end of the file was the wording stamped into it 'NICHOLSON HOLLAND' on the other side also stamped into it were the words 'FLAT BASTARD'. Where did they get that name? I think I owe the ironmonger an apology.

Well, enough of that.

I started filing the cuttlefish bone until it fitted snugly into the top and bottom of the tin. With my knife, I cut a couple of little notches opposite each other; and then went for a coffee. It was all now down to Vesta. At eight fifty-five, I walked into Sydney Street from the Kings Road end. I had only gone a few hundred yards when I saw Vesta ahead of me she was nervously looking over her shoulder; I walked past her waiting for the signal, I had only just past her when I heard her voice.

"Bob."

I walked further down the road and eventually stepped into a doorway. Within a matter of seconds, Vesta joined me; she looked very frightened.

"Bob, I cannot stay long. I have the key." And with that, she opened her jacket and reached into her blouse, fumbled about and brought out the key. It was as she had drawn; rusty and with a sailing ship in full sail on the end of the shank, the lock end was showing areas of clear metal as if it had been used recently. I took out the tin with the cuttlefish bone in it; I gently pressed the key into the soft side of the bone and then eased the lid closed. Opening the lid slowly, I removed the key leaving a perfect impression of the locking end.

Vesta looked in amazement.

"Where did you learn to do that?" She smiled and took the key from me.

"Oh, an old burglar showed me how to copy keys."

She shook her head and replaced the key inside her bra, closed her blouse; fastened her jacket and walked off. I watched as she walked up the staircase to the house entrance; as she did so a black Mercedes car pulled up outside. It was the Mercedes from Dummer.

I hope Vesta had time to replace the key.

I waited in the street for about ten minutes. In the distance, I could see the Mercedes driver smoking as he leant against the bonnet of the car. He suddenly flicked the cigarette into the middle of the road and walked quickly to the side of the car, opened the rear door; two men walked down the steps of the house and climbed into the car. The driver got in and drove off.

I returned home all the time hoping that Vesta had managed to return the key without them finding out.

The following morning, Vesta phoned to tell me that everything was okay and the key was back in the drawer. The men had come and waited for a telephone call from Russia and what she had gathered there was another six girls coming into the UK on Saturday.

The more I thought about what Vesta had said 'they only take the key for two or three hours', I very much doubted if that would have given them time to drive to Braithwaite Manor and return within that time scale and besides that why not hide the key at the Manor. No, this had to be for premises closer to Chelsea but what type of premises would still be using this type of key?

Chapter 13
Where Is the Lock That Fits the Key?

I walked into Wokingham town centre. It was about eight thirty and the town was just coming into life; the local window cleaner and his father were going about their business. I stopped and passed the time of day with them the conversation was interrupted.

"Watch out for that Jock, check his passport before you do anything." It was Pete from the cobblers shop; there was no mistaking his cockney accent. Standing next to him was his wife Trish. She ran the adjoining dry cleaning shop although many of the people in town felt she should have continued her career as a model. Pete a jovial chap, well liked in the area had swept her off her feet a few years earlier and they married. I always teased him that men in town were deliberately soiling their clothes to give them the chance to speak to her.

"Pete, we need to talk. Have you got five minutes?"

"Yeah sure, pop in."

The shop was part of old Wokingham with some of the buildings dating back to the fifteenth and sixteenth century. The shop was now being used as a shoe repairer with facilities for key cutting. One wall was lined with rows of blank keys. I showed him the cuttlefish bone with the key impression set in it.

"Pete, do you know anyone who could make me a key from this impression?"

"You're having a laugh. Of course I do, but he is very expensive. I trained as a locksmith I have my workshop at home, it's a bit of a hobby with me now I love working on antique keys and locks." He took the tin and studied the impression.

"This looks like it is from a Joseph Bramah; he started making locks in seventeen eighty-four, his first shop was in Denmark Street in London and then he moved to One Seven Eight Piccadilly in London a fascinating chap, came from Yorkshire. Can you imagine his first shop in Denmark Street in London and here we are today in Denmark Street in Wokingham, fascinating, truly fascinating."

He stood shaking his head as he stared at the casting.

"This is for a high security lock at a rough guess I would say manufactured by the old master himself, somewhere about eighteen ten."

"Coffee?"

Trish glided into the shop with two mugs of coffee. What a relief. I felt I was going to be in the shop for hours as Pete slipped into his own world of locks.

"Did you know the Egyptians invented locks and it was a Mr Yale who copied them?"

He never got any further; Trish came to my rescue.

"Is he boring you with lock stories? He spends hours in his workshop at home whilst I sit and watch television." She left the shop shaking her head. She was dressed as if she was about to step onto a 'catwalk'.

Pete looked at the mould.

"What type of premises is this lock for?"

"I can't really say. A friend asked me if I could get it done. I think it is a family thing up in Scotland. Give me a call if you have any luck. I'll be around."

"Bob, are you about to screw the Tower of London?"

"Don't worry; you will get your cut if I am."

I left the shop and walked past the dry cleaners. An elderly gentleman was putting a pair of trousers in for cleaning; he was pointing out some stains to her as he bent over the counter. She mouthed over his head, "Dirty Bugger."

I pointed to my chest with my index finger and mouthed back, "Who me?"

She looked directly at me and in a loud voice said, "Yeah, you too."

The elderly gentleman looked up. "Sorry?"

I did not wait for the rest of the conversation but walked off chuckling to myself.

Chapter 14
A Load of Rubbish?

I was aware it would take Pete some time to make me a key assuming of course he could. I had plenty of things to do and most of all I wanted to find out what was in the rubbish at Braithwaite Manor at Dummer. I was sure Violet had said the Russians threw out their rubbish for collection on a Tuesday morning. Over the past years, both in and out of the police, valuable information had been obtained by searching through discarded paper work. I drove down to Dummer in the early hours of Tuesday morning and sure enough stacked outside the gates were a number of black plastic bags. I pulled into a nearby vehicle passing point and walked back to the bags. Groping about in the dark, I could feel the contents of the bags; two or three of the bags contained bottles; the another two felt like the contents were paperwork, and the other, slightly heavier felt like clothing. Grabbing the tops of the bags, I ran off in the darkness keeping watch for any approaching car headlights. This time, I was lucky and made it back to my car without incident. I drove home and left the bags in my car until the following morning; despite having done numerous 'garbology' runs over the years there was always an air of excitement as to what the contents would reveal.

I awakened from my sleep at about seven o'clock, put on my dressing gown and went out to my car, I was like a kid on Christmas morning waiting to open my parcels; I collected the bags and took them into the garage, put down a dust sheet, put on my rubber gloves and emptied the contents onto the sheet. Picking through the paperwork, I tried to put it in some form of order; petrol, restaurant and various parking receipts, always very handy for tracking someone's movements. I put the contents into various plastic bags for future examination. The cartons of discarded food were returned to their original bags. No point reheating the food as there may have been a hair in it; my mind reverted back to sick police humour, I chuckled to myself. Plastic shopping bags fell out first; each was bound over the top with black gaffer tape. I put them to one side and examined the other contents; a large butcher's knife, a hacksaw and a number of what appeared to be blood stained surgical gloves. The Christmas excitement feeling was leaving me.

What the hell am I getting myself into?

I walked into the utility room took off the gloves and washed my hands. It was cup of teatime; after all, I was still in my dressing gown. I ate some cereal and returned to the garage. I looked at the five Tesco bags lying on the floor. They were never intended to be on my garage floor, they were intended to go to the Council incinerator for destruction, never to be seen again.

What secrets did they hold? I picked up my Stanley knife and started to cut the gaffer tape. My phone rang. I walked into the kitchen, and picked up the phone.

"Hello, MacInally."

"Bob? It's Vesta; we must meet. I met Tetyana last night; she wants to meet you. She is very frightened. She thinks something bad has happened to Nadya."

We agreed to meet the next morning at Johnstone's café in the Regent Palace Hotel.

I went back into my garage and cut the gaffer tape and emptied the contents out onto the dustsheet. A pair of what appeared to be a pair of woman's denim jeans fell out. I picked them up. They were small with floral embroidery above the pockets. I put them to one side and opened another bag, turned it upside down and emptied the contents out. A white cotton blouse fell out; I gently opened it, once again, it had an embroidery pattern of flowers sewn above the breast pockets. What appeared to be blood splatters, not a lot just a few streaks were above the sleeves. I tipped out the other contents; a pair of ladies brown high heeled ankle length boots they looked to me as if they were about size three. I put them next to the blouse and as I did so I saw a small piece of screwed up paper in the corner of the pocket it was about the size of a train or bus ticket. Unrolling it, I made out the wording Kyivpastrans along the bottom. The shoes despite being well worn were clean and well-polished. The next two bags contained jumpers and outer clothing. I searched through the pockets; they were empty. The labels inside had the wording Elan Miro on them; was this the former owner? The next bag contained a small rucksack and make-up, perfume, eye shadow, scissors and a hairbrush; with long blonde hairs rolled around it. Screwed up in one of the small inside pockets was an aircraft boarding card for Ukraine International Airlines. I opened it out it was for a flight from Kiev to

London Heathrow in the name of Nadya Davidovich. I tipped out the other three bags. One contained ladies underwear. I felt like a bit of a pervert as I checked the sizes; they were for a slightly built female. The others contained letters addressed to N Davidovich at an address in Kiev, a number of Ukrainian newspapers and magazines were in a stack as if they had been lifted from a coffee table or similar. There was no doubt someone was attempting to destroy the identity of this female.

Where was this person? I had a fair idea who she might be; the question was, is she still alive?

Chapter 15
So, You Are Tetyana

As I crossed the road to the entrance of the Regent Palace Hotel, I saw Vesta standing outside the front doors. As soon as I crossed over to her, she smiled and walked inside. I followed her in.

"Hello, Bob. Tetyana is in the café. She is very frightened; I have told her you are a good man. She has so much to talk about I just hope she trusts you."

Entering the café, Vesta led me over to a tall woman sitting at the central carousel. She had her back to us. Vesta spoke to her in their native tongue. She turned around and stood up off the stool.

"Bob, this is Tetyana; a friend of Nadya."

I reached out and shook her hand. Tetyana was aged about twenty years and about six feet tall. She had a beautiful complexion; no makeup, her long dark hair was tied up beneath a white baseball cap the large sunglasses she was wearing hid her eyes. Large gold rings hung from her ears.

"Hello Tetyana I am pleased to meet you; do you speak English?"

"A little, not good but I understand."

"Let's go and sit in the corner."

I picked up her coffee cup and we walked over to the table. I ushered her into a seat facing the wall and I sat opposite with Vesta. The waitress took our order and after a few minutes, returned and poured out our coffees.

I listened to her story as to how she too had been conned into coming to England on the pretext of modelling but had been forced into being a high-class prostitute for Arabs. She had been made to stay in the flat where Vesta lived, and had been told that she and her friends were going to live on a boat to be with Arab oilmen and she would do whatever they wanted. One day, a little Russian man, the man who drives the car, came to the house and made her have sex with him. There was a fight and she stuck a broken glass in his neck. He punched her so hard that that she was knocked out. When she came around, he was standing over her with a gun in his hand. She said she had not done too much damage to him as he was holding a towel to his neck and there was only a little blood on it. He then put the gun in her mouth and shouted at her that she was going to stay at Mister Walter's house with Nadya.

Through her tears, she described the rest.

"I tried to put my hands up to the gun, but he had tied them together with a belt. He then calls me a dirty Ukrainian whore and tells me to stand up as we were going to Nadya, another bitch, and she would explain to Ukrainian bitches what happens when they don't do what they are told. I stood up and he made me hang my jacket over my hands to cover the belt. He then went to the drawer in the coffee table and took out the big key that Vesta told you about. We then went downstairs to his car and he made me sit in the front seat; he was laughing and kept saying things like 'company for your little friend Nadya'. He told me to shut my eyes and put the chair back till I look at roof. I was frightened but happy I was going to see my friend Nadya. We drive for about half an hour and then we stop at traffic lights and foreign boy says he clean windows of car. The Russian pig says no but he bought a lot of, how you say 'roses' and put them on top of my hands. The flowers were at my nose they had lovely smell and made me think of my home; he starts to laugh and say they should be on top of the box. I pray to myself Jesus help me; he is going to kill me.

We stop at a road with big trees on one side and houses on the other. He tells me 'get out you filthy whore'; I say you make me whore. He just laughs. All the time, I am thinking of my good family at Ukraine. I start to get out of car he takes the belt off my hand and he makes me hold flowers in front of me, like how you say 'a bride lady'. I dropped them on the ground and he say pick them up filthy Ukraine cow. I bend down and start to pick them up. He still laughs, not a normal laugh; a bad man laugh. I start to look up at him; my face is at, how you say 'balls'. I then punched his balls and then took hold of them and twisted them. He screamed and bent down I put my leg in his face. This time, there is much blood from his mouth and nose; he makes big noise and falls on the ground. I ran away, some street boys are laughing at him as I run away. I look around and the boys were taking things from his pockets and then they too run away. It was getting dark. I keep running and then go into big woods and hide under bush. I think I sleep and after a minute, hour, day I don't know, I waken up and there is one of Jesus angels looking over me. I cry and pray. I get up to kiss angel feet. She was made of stone I was in the place where dead people go, what you call it?"

I interrupted.

"A cemetery. Do you remember if this was south or north of the Thames River?"

"I am not sure, but as he drove me in the car I saw the big Parliament clock on the right, how you call it the Big Ben?"

She was shaking. Vesta reached out and held her hands and said a few words in Ukrainian. Vesta tells me that she thinks she has told me too much. Tetyana looked into my eyes, I changed hands with Vesta and gently held Tetyana's hands, they were ice cold.

"Tetyana, have you got a place to stay?"

"Yes, I can stay at my boyfriend's mother's house; she has been very kind."

"I would like to meet with you again, with your boyfriend, okay?"

"Yes, okay, you have met him."

"I have?"

"Yes, he is George the caretaker."

We finished our coffees and went our separate ways; I asked myself so many questions on my return to home. The postman had delivered the usual load of rubbish, as I sifted my way through it I came across a postcard from Liz in Mallorca.

Hi Bob,

I will be in London between the eleventh and sixteenth of next month. I will give you a call and perhaps we can meet up.

Love

Liz x

PS I have stopped drinking!

Chapter 16
Valuable Rubbish

I went into my garage and was immediately greeted by the fusty smell from the salvaged paper work and clothing. Amongst the various pieces of paperwork was a number of petrol receipts all paid for in cash. They showed that whoever was buying the petrol was using a filling station in South London in the Old Kent Road. Not an area where one would choose to go by choice. Was this the route taken by the little Russian man when he was taking Tetyana to see Nadya? And if so, what type of old business was in the area where the key would fit the lock? Were they travelling north or south on the road; going to or coming from the destination? I decided to visit the garage but not before, I would try and have another night out with Elensa. There was only one thing for it go back to the café.

"Good morning, would Mister Bond like a cappuccino?"

"Oh, Elensa, you gave me a fright; it is not good for a man of my age." She had just entered the café and was about to start work.

"I am so sorry, let me take my coat off and I will serve you." She ran into the 'back shop' and reappeared almost immediately putting on her overall.

"Now you go and sit down and I will bring the cappuccino to you."

I sat down and started to read my newspaper.

"One cappuccino with chocolate." I looked up. Once again, that enigmatic smile appeared on her face.

"How are you, Elensa?"

"I am good but I need a favour, yes?"

"What can I do for you?"

"I have an invitation to go to a party at the Latvian Embassy next week, my friend works there and she has sent me two tickets for next Thursday evening. Would you like to come; I don't want to sound cheeky; you understand."

"I have a problem. I am not doing you a favour. It is you that is doing me the favour. Yes, I will be very pleased to come."

We agreed a place to meet the following week. I left the café like a cat who had got the cream. This was better than I had expected.

I set off for The Old Kent Road, not the most desirable location in London; long gone were the Cockney people who a few years before had been proud to say they were from the area. They had long since left as immigrants moved in changing the ancient character of South London that produced people like Henry Cooper the boxer who took most of Britain top boxing prizes. He trained in the Gym above the Thomas a Becket public house. Then there was Tommy Steel, the pop star and actor who became world famous. The road in Roman times had been the main road between Londinium (London) and Rome. It was the Pilgrim route in Chaucer's Canterbury Tales. Tales were told to me by old cops who took me around the area 'learning beats' when I had just started in the police. I remember an old copper who at his retirement party and with the aid of a few pints sang, "Wotcher-Knocked 'em in the Old Kent Road." I remember the chorus.

"Wotcher," all the neighbours cried.

"Who you goin' to meet Bill?"

"Have you bought the street Bill?"

Laugh-Lord I thought I should've died,

I knocked them in the Old Kent Road.

The memories flooded back as I crawled along through the heavy traffic. I opened the car window and listened; gone were the cockney accents. It was now all languages from India and Asia. What would the old Cockneys who had survived the Blitz think of their town now?

I slammed on my brakes narrowly missing the stationery car in front of me. So much for day dreaming, as the reality hit me I saw a filling station ahead of me. Was this the one that had issued the receipts to the Russian? It would follow that if Tetyana had seen 'Big Ben' on her right, she would be travelling south. So, what was the Russian's interest south of the Thames? It had to be a building where they could use the key. I continued down the road and towards the garage and pulled in and bought some petrol. The receipt was identical to the ones from the rubbish. I continued through a couple of sets of traffic lights. I stopped at the next set. There was a guy selling flowers.

"You like some nice roses for the lady?"

He picked some out of the large basket he was carrying and held them to my window. Fortunately, the lights changed and I drove off. Was this the route the little Russian had taken Tetyana?

I pulled over and consulted my map I considered what Tetyana had said. A street with a park on one side and a row of houses on the other, she had wakened up next to an angel, a cemetery maybe?

Why would anyone take a key to a cemetery?

The nearest cemetery I could find in the area was Nunhead. This was at least a mile from where I had stopped, it was worth a try. I started the car engine and made my way towards Linden Grove and the front gates of the cemetery, sure enough the left-hand side of the road was a stonewall with iron railings on the top with trees and bushes; even as the sun shone this was a sinister looking place, its unkempt appearance did nothing to help. On the right-hand side of the road and opposite, the gates were rows of terraced houses.

I walked through the open wrought iron gates and past the six stone pillars towering some twenty feet above me. I walked slowly up the broad avenue to the Anglican chapel at the end. Despite the sun shining, there was an uncanny chill in the air. Plants were covered with green mildew with the residue of the previous year's growth rotting beneath them. No person had taken time to dispose of the dead plants from the previous year's likewise the tombs and memorials dedicated to people long since gone from this world. The Chapel overlooked woodland of Ash and Sycamore trees, which, over the years, had covered the stone angels and gothic tombs. On the right-hand side of the avenue, I noticed a monument dedicated to the Scottish Political Martyrs, as I stood reading the inscriptions I became aware of a man standing next to me.

"Aye you interest in the Martyrs then?"

"Just passing through and stopped to have a look." He looked at me.

"Ah, a Glesga man."

"That's me, and yourself?"

"Aye, 'am a Glesga man came doon here after the war and stayed ever since. Shug!"

His small Skye Terrier came scuttling out of the undergrowth with what appeared to be a forearm bone in its mouth. He reached down and took it from the dog's mouth.

"Sit, stay." The dog sat at his heel.

"Shug's always finding bones. Years ago, grave robbers would dig up the bodies and pinch anything they could find, buggers never put the bones back and wee Shug here finds them and brings them back to me."

With that, he lobbed the bone into the thick undergrowth no doubt for wee Shug to find another day.

And with that, he thrust out his hand.

"Wullie McIntyre." I took hold of his hand and shook his firm grip; unlike the dead fish hand of the guy in Mallorja.

"Bob MacInally, pleased to meet you."

"And you. I always take the dug for a walk through here aboot this time of day, yi widnae want to come in later on, all the wasters and arseholes of the world descend on here, Junkies, lowlife nae use to naebody. In the old days, you could walk through here, the grounds were in good condition, well looked after but no noo. The locals call it a Nature reserve; nature reserve my arse; the only wild animals here have got two legs.

"A few weeks back, I saw a young lassie running in here. She looked terrified. I never saw her leave. I keep thinking I'll find her body. I walked out of the gates and there's four young yobs kicking shit out of a wee guy on the pavement. He could not have been too bad as I saw him get into his car and drive off. The yobs walked off looking at the spoils they had nicked from him: a nature reserve? It's a bloody jungle!"

And with that, he walked off shaking his head.

I had a walk through parts of the cemetery and took some photographs. The area was over run and not been attended for years. The roads that wound their way through were generally in good condition. After I had walked about two hundred yards, I came across an elderly couple attending a grave. They explained the grave belonged to their second or third generation uncle and they said the friends of Nunhead Cemetery were only too pleased to see people making an attempt to clean up the fifty-two-acre cemetery to its Victorian splendour. They were doing their best as they loaded their estate car with weeds and branches they had cut back exposing a headstone which they were in the process of cleaning and returning it to as near its original condition as possible. I am sure their old uncle would be pleased with their efforts as he looked down or up whichever the case may be.

Chapter 17
Roll on Thursday

I processed the pictures of the cemetery and waited for a call from Tetyana or her boyfriend. Whilst waiting, it gave me the opportunity to search through the documents I had received and take a further look through the rubbish from Dummer. The more I thought about things, the more I realised I was getting into deep water. Should I go to the police with what I had? Deep down I knew the police would not be interested in my suspicions and if I was honest with myself, they were pretty flimsy. I had heard it all before; we don't have the budget to investigate this type of thing. Pick up any newspaper and look at the serious cases being thrown out of court because some police officer had made a mistake in their pocket book notes. Nobody seemed to give tinkers curse for the poor victims. Many of them died and what chance did they have to give evidence and tell the true story of what happened and not the concocted one between the accused and their solicitor.

I just hope I am not getting bitter and twisted with what is going on and after all, we can't turn the clock back. But something has got to be done to stop the 'slag' of this world getting the upper hand and walking all over the innocent.

It's Thursday and my date. I have not had what I would call a real date in over a year.

I arrived at Elensa's flat and rang the doorbell. It sounded like an old-fashioned buzzer which vibrated through the door as I pressed it, I pulled my finger off with the shock.

The door opened and there stood Elensa. She gets better looking every time I see her.

"Oh, hi Bob. Come in. I will only be a moment."

She directed me into the lounge area, which was small with everything 'spick and span'. I had just sat down on a white cane chair as I looked around.

After a couple of minutes, I stood up and walked over to a shelf display. The first two shelves had DVDs all stacked in alphabetical order. They were mostly made up of classical music with a small selection of pop albums.

The fragrance of an expensive perfume gently floated into the room, it was scarcely noticeable.

"Okay, I'm ready, when you are."

"You look stunning. Someone will run off with you at this party tonight."

"Well, Mister Bond, that's your job tonight to make sure nobody does."

"Okay that's a deal."

We walked down the stairs to my car. I opened the passenger's door and waited as she got in. I closed the door and walked around to the driver's side and climbed into the driver's seat.

"I like Mercedes cars."

She gently rubbed her hand over the leather seat.

"Does Mister Bond always open the front door for ladies to get into cars?"

"No, I have put a few in the back seat in my time."

"You naughty man."

"No, I meant when I was in the police."

"I understand and you have only very small seats in the back of this car."

She reached over and put her hand on the top of mine as it rested on the automatic gear change. She gave it a gentle squeeze. I looked at her and smiled.

We were soon in London. I parked the car and we made our way to the party.

Drinks were served along with a vast selection of food, some I had never seen before.

"Are you not drinking, Bob?"

"I have to be careful I'm driving."

"That's okay, Svetlana says if you want to stay at her flat you can sleep on her sofa and I can have her spare room, is that a problem?"

"No, not really, I'll have another Champagne please."

Elensa smiled and put her arm around my waist and gave me a none too gentle squeeze.

After a couple of hours, the party finished and Elensa, Svetlana and I made our way to a local pub and passed the night away listening to tales from our various countries until late into the evening when we then made our way back to Svetlana's flat situated on the third floor of a luxury block of Victorian flats just behind The Royal Albert Hall in Kensington. Svetlana pointed out where the coffee and cereals were and then made her apologies explaining she had an early start in the morning and went off to bed. I sat on the settee and after a few minutes, Elensa came over and stretched out next to me with her head on my lap. She closed her eyes as I stroked her hair. Within few minutes, she was sound asleep, followed by me shortly after. Sometime later, an hour or two, I felt her getting up and walking away to return with a duvet and place it over me. I kept my eyes shut as she gently kissed my forehead and went to her bed.

Chapter 18
A Grave Situation

It was seven o'clock when I wakened after what was a surprisingly good sleep. Elensa was up, dressed and had already made coffee.

"Good morning, Bob, did you sleep well?"

"Yes, very well. The settee is very comfortable and thanks for the duvet."

We returned to the car and drove back home. Soon I was dropping off Elensa near her home. She opened the car door and turned around.

"Bob, thank you very much for last night. I had a wonderful night. Thanks for coming with me." I looked at her and smiled.

"No, thank you. It was very kind of you to ask."

She swung her legs out of the car, looked over her shoulder smiling.

"Elensa, thanks for the good night kiss."

"Oh you, you were awake, ah, you are a bad man. I will never understand you English men."

"Elensa, Scottish if you please."

She leaned back, and put her hand behind my neck and pulled my face down to hers and planted a full kiss on my lips. We seemed to be stuck together for ages. Eventually, we slowly parted. She looked up smiled stuck her tongue cheekily out and whispered, "Ah, you did not pretend to be sleeping that time, that's nice."

She got out of the car and walked off waving her hand over her shoulder.

I returned home. There were no messages on my answer machine. I showered, changed and made my way back down to Nunhead Cemetery. I felt sure there had to be a connection with what the Scotsman had said the girl, the yobs, but where did the key fit in this saga? I parked my car and some distance down from the gates and walked up to the Chapel. It was in a bad state of repair; the key certainly was not being used here. I continued searching around for about an hour without success. I was just about to call it a day when I saw a man walking towards me. He looked familiar from the distance. I walked along an unkempt path and crouched between some bushes. He walked past but unfortunately, I could not get a good view of him although he did look the right build for the Russian at the hospital. I followed him from a distance and saw him leave through the gates. By the time I got to the gates, he had gone but a little red car, perhaps a Ford, drove past along Linden Grove. I was convinced the driver was the Russian. This was the connection and I had to find the lock for the key.

I turned back into the cemetery and retraced my steps back to where I had first seen him. The road split into a fork I took the left fork looking for what, I did not know. I eventually found myself in Limesford Road at the south gate. I turned and walked back and turned left, walking back towards the main gate. Very few people were on the road, just the occasional old couple carrying some flowers no doubt to place on the grave of some relative long since laid to rest. I stopped to read a gravestone of some guy by the name of Elliot a Peninsula a war soldier. I rubbed off some of the moss on the stone and discovered he had died in eighteen sixty-three. I stood staring at the stone thinking, who comes to visit this grave now?

I continued on my way puzzling as to why one Russian would come and visit such a place. To visit a long-lost relatives grave? No, not this man. And anyway why bring the key, if in fact he had?

The sound of my shoes suddenly stopped. Looked up and a few yards in front of me on top of a large marble structure, I saw the silhouette of a large sailing ship in full sail. Making my way toward it and through the undergrowth, I eventually reached a small clearing. The ship was on top of a large marble mausoleum. The side and front were partially covered in Ivy. Beneath the Ivy, I read part of the inscription 'HERE LIES SIR WALTER BRATHWAITE, SHIP OWNER, MERCHANT MAN AND BENIFACTURE TO MANY ORPHANAGES THROUGH OUT THE BRITISH EMPIRE ALSO, LADY VICTORIA ANNA BELLE BRAITHWAITE HIS BELOVED WIFE'.

On the front of the tomb was carved a sailing ship in full sail. I was surprised to see the one on top of the roof had lasted so long then again unlike the others I had seen this one appeared to be cast iron. This had to be old Walter's resting place and what a resting place, many a person would be happy for this as their home; it was a 'small bungalow'. I walked around the other side and inscribed on this wall the inscription read; HERE LIES WALTER STANLEY

BRAITHWAITE SON OF THE LATE LORD AND LADY BRAITHWAITE. DIED FOR HIS COUNTRY. Beneath this were the words of The Navy Hymn.

> Eternal Father, strong to save,
> Whose arm both bound the restless wave,
> Who bidst the mighty ocean deep
> Its own appointed limits keep
> O, hear us when we cry to Thee
> For those in peril on the sea!

Was this Mister Stanley's' house, a tomb? I walked to the rear a flight of stairs led down to what appeared to be a basement area. Dead leaves covered the ten steps. I guardedly walked down one step at a time. Cobwebs covered the ornate walls with carved angels looking heavenward each with their hands held as if in prayer. Where I was holding on, I notice that cobwebs were missing from that area. Some person or persons had recently had put their hands on the cold damp stone I was now touching. At the bottom of the stairs and below ground level was a large metal door; it looked that over the years people had tried to force it open without success, likewise the ornamental pull handle. I examined the door; on the right-hand side was a large keyhole.

Was this the lock that Stanley's key would fit, and if it did, why would any person want to visit a tomb?

I walked back to my car and returned home. I had to get the copy of that key.

Chapter 19
Will It Fit?

The following morning, I strolled into Wokingham for my usual shot of caffeine.

"Good morning, Bob, what did you do to Elensa the other night. I have not seen her so happy in ages?" It was Sue; she handed me my coffee.

"Me?"

"Yes, you, she has told me about the wonderful night she had and the only bit I didn't believe, she said you were the perfect gentleman. Now that I found hard to swallow."

"Sue, I get the name but I'm not getting the game."

"Go and sit down and enjoy your coffee. Oh, by the way, Pete from the cobblers was in looking for you yesterday."

I finished my coffee and walked up to the cobblers. As usual, Pete was repairing shoes for some people who had brought in shoes that should have been thrown out but expected him to work miracles, which he frequently did.

"There you are, my dear. You should get another fifty years out of them, that'll be seven pounds fifty." He dropped the shoes into a brown paper bag, and the old lady, I guess aged about seventy-five years walked out of the shop with a broad smile on her face. He looked at me.

"How I make a profit I will never know? I try to keep the old dears happy and you never know I may be mentioned in their will. I'll bet she will bring in another pair to me for heeling in the afterlife. By the way, I have your key. I hope it fits."

He reached under the counter and brought out the new key, a shining steel copy.

"I put a long shank on it with a 'T' bar to turn it. I guessed that it would be for a very thick door, so don't force it when you try to turn it or you may damage the lock."

"How much do I owe you?"

"Have that on me, I'll have one of the diamonds out of the crown jewels once you have nicked them."

I left the shop and bought a few bottles of good wine from the nearby Off License shop. I took them back to Pete.

"Pete, here is a little something until I get the jewels."

Trish had just come out of the back shop. She looked into the carrier bag, saw the wine, picked up the bag and started to walk out of the shop.

"Cheers, Bob, that will pay for all the nights I sat on my own when he was playing in his workshop."

With that, she walked out of the shop. Pete stood, mouth open his hands held forward with the palms turned upwards. He despondently shook his head.

I left the shop, the key burning a hole in my pocket. I had to find if the key would work.

I drove into London and down to the cemetery. I left my car in a nearby street and walked to the cemetery gates. The sun was shining as I walked through the gates. The sinister chill remained and appeared to get even more spine chilling the further I walked into the cemetery. The shadows of the overhanging trees seemed to dance a bizarre ghost like dance.

I was getting frightened, an experience not felt in years. Did carrying the key cause this feeling; a potential house-breaking implement or was it just this place?

I would soon find out. Walking down the steps to the door of the Mausoleum, I had checked the surrounding area prior to going down the steps. Convinced there was no person in the area but still the feeling of being watched remained. Cautiously walking down the stairway and eventually reaching the paved area, I looked back. Nobody was there. I removed the key from my pocket and gingerly inserted it into the lock and started to turn it slowly. There was a little resistance at first and then it completed a full turn and stopped. I reached out and took hold of the ornate handle and pulled. The door slowly opened. I removed the key and pulled the door fully open. The daylight rushed in and spiders scurried away into their hiding places. I looked into the darkness. There was a further flight of stairs leading into what looked like the bowels of the earth. I looked in and was tempted to go down but suddenly the thought came to me. What happens if the door closed behind me?

No problem. After all, I have a key; I checked for the internal keyhole. There was none, then again residents here were never intended to leave, this was their last resting place.

My eyes were getting used to the dark. Straining, I looked further down, sitting on a step was a torch. I picked it up and switched it on the beam was bright, suggesting the batteries inside were new. Directing the beam down into the stairwell revealed a red ornamental rope handrail threaded through brass loops attached to the wall. Pulling the door up behind me, things became more sinister. Someone had tied the rope on the opposite side of the stairs to a ship's wheel, which had been fixed to the inside of the door. I pulled on the wheel and the door gently shut. One end of the rope was tied to one of the brass loops the other end slipped over the wheel spokes and kept the door shut. In some way, I felt more secure once I had done it, but how on earth do you feel secure in a cold tomb?

The torch beam lit my path as I went down the stairs to a bottom chamber. The air was very cold but in a strange way fresh. I walked in and wiped cobwebs from my face.

What the torch beam picked up was the last thing I expected to find. A number of car batteries were sitting on the ground each linked to the other with wires. Two wires led up the wall and stopped. Hanging from above were an identical pair of wires. I reached up and joined them, red to red and black to black, I blinked as the chamber was lit by a series of little bulbs.

The area measured approximately twelve feet long by eight feet wide; the vaulted ceiling was in the region of twenty feet high. On either side of the chamber from the floor were stone shelves about three inches thick and about three feet wide running the full length of the chamber. Each supported by ornamental stone brackets with the names of the deceased carved into the edge of the shelves. Three coffins rested on their allotted shelves. Each lid had a brass plate on top. The lids had been opened and were left askew on top of the open coffin. I rubbed the dust off the nameplate with my bare hand and read it, it was Stanley's' coffin; I moved the lid to one side and shone the torch in. The coffin lining had started to disintegrate. Resting in the bottom was the skeleton of Stanley, still dressed in his now disintegrating captain's uniform complete with his cap, which was now lying at a jaunty angle on his skull. The pockets of his uniform had been ripped open.

The next coffin contained the remains of Victoria. She was dressed in what had been a long white silk dress that had started to rot exposing her rib cage. All the features of her face had long since gone leaving the skull with the eye sockets in some way staring at me. Three pearls lay next to the top of her spine. Had the thief missed them as he ripped the strand of pearls from her earthly remains?

In the third coffin were the remains of Walter. He too was now a skeleton and had been laid to rest in his morning suit. On the faded waistcoat was the distinct mark of a chain, presumably a watch chain. The marks led to where a pocket had been but now sadly this had been ripped off to get to the pocket watch. I replaced the coffin lids to the position I had found them. On the floor in the corner was a couple of large plastic boxes and something covered over by canvas sacking, also a plastic bin liner taped at the top with black gaffer tape similar to the bags I had taken from Braithwaite house.

I felt I had spent enough time in this place. I felt I was intruding on sacred ground. Apparently, this had not troubled the people who had put in a lighting system albeit a very primitive one. Why?

I disconnected the lighting system and made my way up the staircase using the torch. Undoing the rope, I slowly opened the door and replaced the torch, got out and locked the door, as I did so I pushed the leaves against the bottom of the door. The thought went through my mind had anyone been outside looking at the tomb door and seeing it open they would now be a long way off and still running. Enough time for these thoughts. I had to get away from the cemetery.

I arrived back at my car, flopped into the driving seat and let out a sigh, had I really spent the last forty minutes' underground in a tomb with three skeletons?

One thing for sure I now knew where Mister Stanley's watch had come from, but what was under the sacking and what was in the plastic boxes? I knew I had to make at least one further visit. These people whoever they are would not have set up the place with the rope 'lock', and would certainly not have put in a lighting system just to rob a few graves. No, there was a lot more to this.

Chapter 20
Should I Go Back?

I arrived back into Wokingham and went straight to the café Elensa came over and served me.

"Good afternoon, Bob, where have you been?"

"Just doing a little work."

"A little work, have you seen your hair?"

I looked into a nearby mirror. Cobwebs. My hair was covered in cobwebs.

"Bob, I thought I made your hair grey. Maybe I frightened you the last time I left."

"No, no nothing like that. I had to get a book out of my loft before I came out. Would you like to come to my place for dinner tonight, do you like duck?"

"I love duck but I don't know where you live."

"I will come and collect you at seven thirty, okay?"

"Yes, that's nice. I will be ready for you."

I finished my coffee and left, time to buy a cookbook and some ingredients and find out how to cook a duck in orange sauce. What made me say that? I've never cooked a duck in my life.

Entering 'Bookends', our local bookshop, I searched along the seemingly endless rows of cookbooks. I was assisted by one of the girls and after some discussions I left with the book that would solve all my problems. I read through a few recipes, some required boiling bones to make a stock. Not for me, I had seen enough bones for one day, thank you. Time to get the ingredients; I had the Port and Orange Liqueur. That was the easy part. After a while, I had had the rest, duck, four oranges, two pounds of butter and so it went on. I arrived home and started to lay out the shopping.

I had a shower, shaved and got the after-shave out; more decisions. Someone once told me never to wear after-shave when you are cooking. Anyway, I got everything ready and drove down into town and collected Elensa. She was waiting, and as usual, she was elegantly dressed. She got into the car and gave me a 'peck' on the cheek. For one who had spent the morning in a tomb, I felt myself shaking; I must be losing my touch.

Elensa sat down on the settee and I poured her a glass of Chateauneuf du Pape. I poured one for myself and we clinked our glasses. I knew by the way she looked at me this meal could so easily be burnt if I didn't get into the kitchen pretty quick. As it happened, the meal turned out pretty good and we spent the night sipping wine in front of the fire. A few kisses were exchanged; was it the wine or was it just Elensa? I was sure it wasn't the wine.

"Elensa, are you happy, I mean are you okay with the wine?"

"Of course I am, I have not been this happy for so many years." She ran her fingers through my hair.

"Don't you like me, Bob?"

I do not remember the rest of the conversation as we walked to my bedroom. It was three o'clock when we wakened.

"Do you mind if I stay until the morning?" She lay there with the sheet held up to her top lip; her eyes smiled. I put my arm under her head and pulled her towards me.

"What do you think?"

She closed her eyes and whispered, "That's nice."

I reached over and switched off the bedside light.

Chapter 21
Can I Go Alone?

This would have been the type of job I would have loved to have got my teeth into when I was a serving officer. Today things were different. The 'force' had changed beyond all recognition. It was no longer a 'force' but was now a 'service'. Who it was serving, I had to wonder. I could not walk into a Police Station and speak to an officer I would end up trying to explain events to the 'civvy' behind the counter and I was in no doubt I would have ended up getting myself arrested for grave robbing or whatever. Then there was the blood-stained clothing in my garage. No, I will carry on and see if I can get some evidence together but that meant another visit to the Mausoleum. The best time to do this would be during the hours of darkness and that would mean hiding in the cemetery until the gates were closed. It was highly unlikely the little Russian guy would go there at night. I drove down to South London, parked well away from the cemetery and walked the rest of the way. There were plenty of overgrown areas where I could hide until darkness fell. It was about ten o'clock when I gingerly crawled out of the undergrowth and walked towards the Mausoleum. I walked on the outside edge of my shoes to reduce the sound from them on the gravel roadway. About one hundred yards from 'Stanley's' house, I crawled into the bushes and stood hidden by a large tree. I was aware of the sound of a male and female talking and giggling. It was a young couple aged about seventeen years of age. They stopped some five yards from me and got into a tight embrace, passionate kissing and exciting groping each other. It didn't take long before her jumper was up around her neck and her bra was off.

"No, not here. Someone may see us." I don't know who she was expecting to be there at this time of night. Little did she know someone was already standing close by.

"Okay, over here."

By now, his trousers and boxers were around his ankles and he shuffled like a demented penguin to the other side of the roadway with her holding his outstretched hand as she hopped on one leg in an attempt to remove her pants which were around one of her ankles. They stumbled to the other side of the road attempting to kiss as they did so this was no doubt an alcohol passion filled evening. On reaching a raised grave slab, he lifted her onto it, throwing her pants onto a low bush. He then climbed up and they indulged in frantic and loud love making on the grave of the appropriately named grave. R.I.P DON COCKER. Eighteen Twenty to Eighteen Sixty-Nine.

After a few minutes, they clambered off, got dressed and walked back in the direction they had come from. I was so tempted to give them a round of applause but thought better of it. Once they were out of sight, I climbed out of my hiding place and made my way to Walter's. The air was warm. I could feel the sweat on my forehead. This I was sure was caused by the fear of what I was about to do. After all, I was about to carry out an illegal act plus I was carrying the key. As I approached the pathway leading to the tomb door, I stopped and listened for any sounds, a screaming fox shattered the still of the late evening. I switched on my torch as I made my way down the staircase. The dead leaves were still against the door this in itself was a worry to me as it meant that when I entered I would leave a clear signal on the ground outside that the door had recently been opened. I took the key from my waistband and put it in the lock and turned it gently trying not to make any noise. The moonlight cast spine-chilling shadows in front of me as I guardedly pulled the heavy door open. My torch's beam lit up the stairs. My heart was pounding in my chest as I stepped inside slowly pulling the door shut behind me. I tied the rope to the ship's wheel and the stood still for a moment as I shook. Was it nerves or was it the cold dry musty air from inside the place where only the dead should be? Starting to walk down the stairs, I flicked the beam around the area and eventually found the wires connected to the car battery; bringing the two ends of the wire together, the area lit up. I stood still as I surveyed the scene. The coffins were as I had left them. To my left were the shelves intended for the arrival of long departed members of the Braithwaite family. For some reason, they had never arrived. I reached down to the two large plastic containers and was about to lift the lid when I thought better of it and took a pair of latex gloves from my jacket pocket and put them on. I looked around; my eyes were becoming accustomed to the lighting. There were more things in here than I had realised. I reached down and lifted the lid off the first box. There was no mistaking the contents. It was slabs of compressed Heroin; each slab sealed in polythene. There was a vast fortune in this box. Replacing the lid, I opened the other box it too was filled with about the same amount there had to be Heroin valued at millions of pounds on the street. What was I getting myself into? I felt like running back up the stairs and getting out of this place, slamming the door behind me and never coming back. My heart was racing; I was in a cold sweat. I wanted to walk out but my feet were glued to the floor. I looked down at the floor. Underneath one of the shelves was a number of canvas sacks, and they were obviously covering something. I reached down and gingerly lifted the corner of one of the sacks. Stacked beneath the edge of the sacks. I looked in disbelief at the stack. It was gold ingots. I folded the rest of the sacks back revealing fifty, one hundred or more bars? How many I did not know but having seen ingots recovered after a robbery at Heathrow Airport, I was aware there were millions of pounds worth gold sitting in front of me. I picked up one of the bars and examined it; there was no Assay mark or company name embossed on the surface. This bar had no markings on it. I placed it back on the stack and shone my torch on the rest; these too were unmarked. I ran my hands over the bars. They were rough and did not have the smooth surface of legitimate gold bars. These had been smelted possibly with a copper penny or glass added and then poured into a chosen mould. This then gives the bar a new identity and a different chemical make-up. I felt the cold biting into me as I looked around. Another canvas sack was wrapped around something; I picked it up, it was heavy, I laid the package out on top of the gold bars and unfolded the sacking. Inside was an Uzi machine pistol complete with four loaded magazines and a suppressor; a number of Latvian passports were wrapped in a plastic shopping bag. I put everything back in place and extinguished the lights and made my way up the staircase. Switching off my torch, I untied the rope and gently opened the door and squeezed out closing the door behind me and into the fresh air. Pushing the leaves and rubbish back into place, I continued up the outside staircase. Looking to my right as I reached ground level, a pair of eyes were staring at me from about six feet away. I froze, the bushes crashed apart and a fox ran off. That was when I discovered adrenalin is brown. I removed my gloves and put my torch back in my pocket and made my way to a gap in the fencing and back to my car and home.

It was three o'clock when I lay down in bed and tried to get some sleep; it did not come easy as the recent events ran through my head.

Chapter 22
A Changed Liz

I jumped with a start as the phone rang. It was nine thirty. I had overslept. Fumbling with the handset, I answered the caller.

"Good morning, Bob, how are you?"

"Liz, good morning; how are you?"

"I'm fine. You sound as if you have had a hard night."

"A bit of a late one; working."

"I'm in London. It would be nice to see you again. Any chance we could meet up?"

I agreed to meet her the following morning. She suggested we met at the coffee shop in the Salvation Army in Oxford Street in London. This was a changed Liz; not the usual boozer to meet. I hoped she had not gone all 'holy' on me.

I walked into my kitchen, made a coffee and strolled in to the lounge and switched on the television news. There was the all too familiar scene of an area cordoned off with police blue tape with a number of police officers in the background searching what appeared to be a council tip. I turned up the sound on the TV just in time to hear the end of the reporter's commentary.

"We will bring you any further news as we get it and in the meantime from Basingstoke, I shall return you to the studio and leave the police as they continue their gruesome search for any further human remains after the discovery of the severed head of a female."

I waited for the news to be repeated an hour later. When it did come back, on it transpired that whilst a refuge cart was tipping its load in the depot one of the workers had noticed some waste, which he considered, was worth investigating. It was at this point he found the severed head in a plastic bag. Police were releasing very little details at the time other to say they believed that the person was female and aged between twenty and thirty years.

Could this be a connection with the girls at Dummer, and most of all, was there a connection with the blood-stained clothing in my garage?

I walked down to the local café and picked up a paper and thumbed through it as I drank my coffee. The paper was full of the usual, people being arrested for serious offences, appearing in court and walking out with a fine or suspended sentences or even worse community service; they laugh all the way home. Does anyone give a toss for the victims? I remember one job I did when I was working on my own; three guys were nicked for stealing cases of booze from their employer. The pleaded guilty at court and were given community service. Due to the fact, the man responsible for the project had nothing for them to do he sent them unsupervised to the British Museum for the afternoon; British justice, this can't go on. How many more criminals will go home laughing whilst the victims and their relatives are scarred for life?

My thoughts turned to Vesta that poor girl, miles from home and raped by some guy who had discarded her like some cigarette end thrown out of a car window never to be given a second thought. Something had to be done about these people, but who was going to do it and give them the justice they deserved?

I made my way to the local train station and on to Waterloo Station in London. On my arrival at the station, I walked across the bridge over the River Thames and making my way towards the West End of London. I walked up Regent Street and stood at the junction of Oxford Circus. Turning left, I saw the Sally Army flag flying a couple of hundred yards on my left.

Making my way to the front door past the welcoming signs, I was directed to the café. Groups of people of all ages were sitting at the tables talking and laughing with each other, there was a 'buzz' about the place. As I looked about, Liz stood up from a table and shouted to me, "Bob, over here."

I walked over to the table where she was sitting with another three women aged between thirty to forty years. I was introduced to them. One, Suzanna was an accountant and the other two, Barbara and Hillary doctors at a London hospital. Two of the three were members of the Salvation Army. Liz produced a cup of coffee and a home-made cake.

"This is Bob; my drinking partner in Mallorca when I was 'on the sauce', he's an Ex-cop so behave yourselves."

"So what do you do now, Bob?" Hillary asked.

"Not a lot. I'm retired now." I hadn't the heart to tell her I seem to have spent the last few weeks creeping around a cemetery and spending time with three dead bodies in a tomb.

"Where do you work, Hillary?"

"Oh, I'm at A and E at Saint Thomas'; do you know it?"

"Yes, I had the pleasure of your services a few years ago." Before I could finish, Liz interrupted.

"Bob was shot when he was in the Police."

"Yes, that was a while ago; Saint Thomas' did so much for me. I'll always be grateful to them. How long have you been there?"

"About three years. I'm now going out to Africa as a volunteer with the 'Army'. We have got hospitals out there and I am leaving in two weeks. Sorry I can't spend more time with you. I have got to go; things to do."

The three women got up said their good byes and left. Liz looked at me and shook her head.

"How I wish I could be going with her; I heard her talking at an 'Army' meeting one day. How she was giving up everything to help the less fortunate in the world. It was as a result of what she said and the influence of Major Mary, you remember I talked about her?"

"Yeah, she was the one who helped you when you had all your grief."

"That's her. She keeps in touch with me and tells me she prays for me each day. Well, I have joined the Salvation Army and am helping in their campaign to help people who are the victims of human trafficking, and as you know Bob, I have first-hand experience of that. You know it's funny how things work out. Who would have thought a few years ago I would be doing this? All this change brought about by one caring person. They could help so many more people but it is the shortage of funds. Anyway, enough about me; how are you and did you ever find that girl in Mallorca?"

"No, I found her friend but Nadya is still missing. Anyway, I'll keep trying, maybe your friend will send up a few prayers for her."

"Well, Bob, it worked for me. I know I am a different person now; it's strange how so much good can come out of badness I just wish I could have found this life before."

"Liz, you have got so much to offer girls who are forced into your old life style. You most of all understand that."

"Bob, I pray every day that I can help them. Who would have thought a tart from the streets of Liverpool could be doing this. As people have said to me, God works in mysterious ways. It's a funny old world. I remember some geezer preaching in a pulpit telling the people that in the Bible God had said the hairs on your head were numbered. I thought what a load of rubbish. Two days later, I'm reading a magazine article about a court case in America where some guy had been done for raping a young girl. As usual, he was denying it until the prosecution produced his DNA which proved beyond a shadow of doubt it was him. The prosecution said the chances of two people having the same DNA was one in ten billion. Made me think about the preacher's two or three-thousand-year-old story about the hairs on our heads being numbered."

I spent another hour with her talking about our lives; Liz had changed not only physically; she must have lost two stones but she had something about her and it didn't come out of a bottle. As I was leaving, she handed me a post card with a picture of a 'blood and fire' flag on the front. I presumed it was a Sally Ann flag. On the rear, she had written;

'Good luck, Bob. I hope you find your lady'. Beneath this she had written 'Psalm 72 verses 12–14'. I put the card in my inside jacket pocket and walked off with so many thoughts in my mind.

Chapter 23
A Head Start

The national papers carried the story of the discovery of the severed head being found in the council tip in Hampshire each had its own take on it. Was it a ritual killing, or was there a psychopath running wild in the South of England?

A senior detective appeared on television appealing for any person with information to come forward or any person with information on any missing female aged between twenty to twenty-five years to come forward. All information would be treated in the strictest of confidence.

Did the blood-stained clothing and the tools have any connections? I was going to be careful from now on or I could find myself facing getting nicked for murder. I had to think of a way to make sure that the 'slag' at Dummer got their 'just desserts'. I hadn't heard from Vesta for some time, I decided to give her a call.

"Hello?"

"Vesta?" Silence.

"Vesta, it's Bob."

"Oh! Hi, Bob, nice to hear from you."

"I thought I would give you a call to see how you are?"

"Things are just the same. They still will not give me my passport and last week, they made me spend two nights with some Arab men in a big hotel in Park Lane in London. They have got more girls over from Latvia this time. When I saw them, they looked very frightened. The big fat Arab, you remember Ameer who smokes the big cigar?"

"Yes, from the big house."

"Yes, that's the one. He was with them. He looked at me and laughed."

"Yes, I remember the man, the one you want to kill."

"Yes, that is the man and now I want to kill him even more."

"Is Tetyana still okay?"

"Maybe, I will tell you if we meet, you understand?"

"Yes, I understand; perhaps we can meet soon. I could meet you tomorrow at the wine bar, you know?"

"Yes, I know, what time?"

"Two o'clock outside."

"Yes, I see you then." She hung up.

I knew enough about the way people talked when they thought their phone was being intercepted. Was the Russian and his friends tapping Vesta's phone. If so, I must warn her about phoning me from the house phone; had they already got my number since the last time she called me? No doubt they had the means to get my home address from the numbering. I did not like the thought of that.

Chapter 24
Time to Play Dirty

Sitting at the terrace outside Gordons wine bar in Watergate Walk, I studied one of the waitresses as she walked past. She fitted nicely into her tight black tee shirt with the white lettering of Gordons Wine bar pointing forward and slightly upwards as she walked amongst the plastic tables picking up the used wine glasses and returning them inside to the bar. A number of city workers were on the table opposite me; they were finishing off yet another bottle of Laurent Perrier Brut NV Champagne. One of the 'lads' replaced the upturned bottle in the silver ice bucket whilst beckoning the waitress with his other hand and ordering yet another bottle. These guys were rich brokers from the City of London spending money as if it wasn't going out of fashion. Their bonuses were in millions of pounds and this drinking session was but a drop in the ocean to them.

After ten minutes, Vesta arrived.

"Hi, Bob, sorry I am late. Some men came to the flat and I was told to make tea and coffee for them. There were four of them. The little Russian man who uses the key was there. He is boss man. He tells me get in other room but I hear them talk about gold and I think drugs. I did not hear everything but they are going to meet Arab men with a big boat I think in Spain; he says they must have new girls to go on boat."

"When did they say they would go to Spain?"

"I did not hear but they did say they would be, how you say, supplying them with lots of young girls to go sailing, they talked a lot about gold and lot about Charlie. I don't know this man Charlie, do you?"

"No, but I think Charlie may be their name for cocaine."

"I heard the two men asking if I could be trusted."

"The Russian just laughed and said something about he hoped so, for my family's health in Russia. I am so frightened for my family. When they had finished, he called me and told me to make tea and coffee for his friends. When I brought it in on a tray, he smacked my bottom and asked the men if they wanted to have me. I thought I was going to put the tray on his head, yes you understand?"

I walked to the bar and ordered a bottle of white wine and two glasses along with some French bread and a selection of cheese and pate. When I arrived back at the table, we picked up the conversation where I had left off.

"Yes, I understand." I could feel the rage building up inside me. Who the hell did this little shit think he was?

"Vesta, I want to find out as much as I can about these people and what they will be doing over the next few weeks. Would you allow me to come to the flat and hide a transmitter, you understand a bug and I will find out what they are doing?"

"This would be very dangerous if they found out, yes?"

"Yes, but I would only be in the house for five minutes, I could do it at night. Think about it and let me know but don't use the house phone in case they are listening to your calls."

I handed her an envelope with three phone cards and one hundred pounds in it.

"Now you take this and call me but remember only from a telephone box."

She took the envelope and looked in it.

"This is too much money. I can't take this from you."

"Yes, you can. It will mean you can talk to your family at home and don't forget to tell them everything is okay."

"I speak to them and tell them I am still doing modelling work. They say we never see your pictures, why? I just say they are for English magazines. If you can put the, how you say 'bug in' and they will not find it can you do it on a Sunday morning about seven o'clock?"

"Yes, I can be there at that time. Are you sure they will not be there?"

"Yes, they never come in the morning. I will put my doll in the window if it is okay to come in, yes?"

"Yes, I understand." We finished our wine and stood up from the table. Vesta came around to me and put her arms around me and kissed be on both cheeks.

"Thank you, Bob, you are a very kind man. Tetyana is safe and is living with the caretaker's mother. He too wants to kill the men who did the terrible things to her." And with that, she walked off towards Charing Cross railway station.

'A very kind man', if only she knew what I was planning.

After a few minutes, I left and made my way home to look out some equipment. I had used this piece before. Invented by Mossad, the Israeli secret service. When fitted to a target telephone, it meant that when the number was dialled from any phone in the world, the handset became live and would pick up any conversation within the room and likewise any telephone conversations. The Israeli had another use for it. They would fit an explosive device into the handset and when their target answered the phone, they would send a signal to the target phone which in turn triggered the explosive and that would blow the persons head off. I only wanted information at this stage.

I collected the equipment from my safe deposit box at Barclays bank in Wokingham and took it home for testing. It was in working order all I had to do was fit it in the flat in Chelsea.

The following morning, I arrived in Chelsea at about six o'clock and parked my car some distance from the flat. The town was quiet, until the wailing of the fire engines sirens as they pulled away from Chelsea Fire Station shattered the peace. A late night reveller, still in his dinner suit from the night before. His jacket slung over his shoulder and the bow tie which no doubt had been tied to perfection the previous evening now hung around either side of his open dress shirt was strolling down the road occasionally changing his step into some form of dance routine. His lady friend's high-heeled shoes were swinging in his hand as she walked barefooted with him. She was still dressed in her evening dress although her dishevelled hair was all over the place, her make up smudged over her face. A bottle of champagne in her hand was being put to her lips as the fire engine pulled out of the station. She raised the bottle and saluted the fire crew. They in turn somehow made their siren give a hoot and the crew cheered as they struggled to get into their kit. Presumably, they were going to the scene of some fire whilst the lovers were going home to turn up the heat.

I walked past the flat and as planned, the doll was sitting at the window as if beckoning me over. No sooner had I climbed the stairs and pressed the button on the entry system, the latch clicked open and I was inside and sprinting up the stairs and through the ready opened door to the flat, Vesta gently closed the door behind me.

"I saw you cross the road. I have been worried in case the Russian man was near. How long will it take to work on the phone?"

She was terrified.

"Take the doll from the window and keep looking out and if you see anything call out to me." I started to undo the bottom of the phone and looked for the all too important screws to connect the very small transmitter to. As I looked at the inside at the mass of transistors, my mind started to race, was it red wire to red or black or was it the reverse. I was getting worried should the Russian arrive and find the phone in pieces. Eventually, I got myself together and made the connections. I replaced the bottom plate and wiped my fingerprints off the cradle and handset. Replacing my tools back in my pocket, I looked at Vesta.

"All done, they will not know any difference. The phone will work as normal. I will go now as soon as I put my tools away."

I put the toolset in my pocket and blew Vesta a kiss. She left the window and opened the door for me. I stepped outside and had reached the bottom when I heard her call my name, I looked up she was standing on the landing.

"He's here outside. Hide."

I looked around for a hiding place and as I did so a door opened behind me and I was pulled backwards into a room and the door slammed shut.

Chapter 25
Things Are Taking Shape

"You silly bastard, you were almost caught. First rule in the Army, have someone cover your back."

I was in the caretaker's flat and there was George smiling at me.

"Cup of tea? I saw you coming in and I thought to myself, the old bugger has still got it in him, slipping into Vesta's for an early morning quickie, only joking. As I looked out of my window, I saw the little Russian shit pull up in his car. I was just about to run upstairs to warn you when I heard Vesta and then I saw you. You had better lie low here until he's gone."

We sat talking. George telling me some 'war stories'. There was no doubt he missed the army life. After a while, he got up from his chair and opened a drawer, took out a small medal box and opened it and handed it to me: inside was his George Medal. He reached over and removed the medal from its box and handed it to me. Around the edge, his name was inscribed.

"Yeah, the good old days. I miss them when I speak to my mates now. Some of them have just come back from Northern Ireland and they tell me stories of what that so-called Republican Army is doing. I would cheerfully go over there and 'slot' some of these cowardly bastards. How brave do you have to be to walk into a pub and leave a bag under a table, walk out and let the bag blow up and kill young innocent people and blow bits off the rest of the others? Pity Mad Mitch is not about, he sorted that type of person out in the Crater district of Aden. He was a Lieutenant-Colonel in the Argyll and Sutherland Highlanders, the Argyll's, your lot, Jocks. When the politicians were sitting in London with their fingers up their arse or their chum's, Mad Mitch as he was known went into the district accompanied by fifteen bagpipers playing Scotland the brave. I have no regrets about leaving a leg in the Falklands that was a battle. The world is going mad. The politicians are scared of their own bloody shadows and lining their own pockets. Take this little Russian shit that visits upstairs. What's his game, does anyone care? The old bill could nick him, what will happen? I'll tell you, he'll be bailed and then he will piss off to Russia never to be seen again. Sorry, I'm rabbiting on."

"No, I understand. It must be very difficult for you a trained, as an um."

"Killer, go on say it cause that what we were, I was due to go to Hereford to be trained but one legged SAS Troopers are no use to them. I would be as much use as a one-legged tap dancer. Another tea?"

"Yeah, cheers." And with that, George got up from his chair and put the kettle on looking out of the window as he did so.

"That's the little Russian leaving; you wait and see he'll be back in a couple of hours. Waits for five minutes and then pisses off, not to be seen for a few days. I fancy following him some day just to see where he goes to."

"No, I wouldn't do that in case he susses you. That would take a bit of explaining particularly with Tetyana being where she is."

"Yeah, I suppose you are right. She's a lovely kid. My mother adores her. But the poor kid is terrified. She has never told my mother what happened to her. Tea's up."

And with that, George handed me a mug of tea. We sat talking for another hour or so.

"One of the old Colonels has set up in business. He supplies men for protection work all over the word. All the guys he uses are ex-mob they get some really good work. It takes them all over the world. They do private work for foreign governments. Two of my old mates tell me they wear white hats and get rid of the bad men who wear the black hats. I was thinking of employing them to get rid of the little Russian guy but I can't afford their prices. Talking about the little Russian guy that's him back. Give him five minutes and he'll be off again."

After about five minutes, George stood up.

"That sounds like Vesta's door closing." He got up and walked over to the window and looked out.

"Yep, as I thought that's him leaving; you would think he would have a better car than that clapped out old B reg. red Ford he drives. I wonder where he lives?"

I didn't pick him up on his question but stood up, placed my mug on the table and walked over to George and shook his hand.

"Thanks for the tea. I must shoot off now and meet up with some friends. I might have some work for your old Colonel."

"If you have the money, he can undertake all jobs and I mean all jobs."
I left Chelsea and made my way home.
'And I mean all jobs'. Did he mean what I thought he meant?

Chapter 26
Good Night Bad News

As soon as I arrived home, I tried out the listening device to make sure it was working. I dialled the flat telephone number and sent a signal down the line. The microphone on the other end 'kicked in' and I could hear the sounds from within the room. That evening, I had a meal with Elensa. It was a wonderful evening and a million miles away from all the grief I felt I was getting myself into. I was beginning to wish I had never picked 'that book' off the shelf. After a couple of glasses of wine, I felt I was beginning to lighten up. Elensa looked at me in a quizzical manner.

"What is wrong, Bob? You do not seem to be your normal self. Don't you want to see me again?"

"No, no it is nothing like that. I am just a bit exhausted. I am working on a job and I am not sure if I am doing the correct thing. Deep down, I think I am but it is so difficult, but being me, I just want to get to the bottom if it and reach a successful end whenever that might be. I can stop any time but I feel I would be letting people down. People are doing bad things and they never seem to be punished properly. Anyway, enough about me. How have you been?"

"I am fine. I was worried you did not want to see me again."

I reached across the table and held her hands, she was crying.

"Bob, it is so difficult when you are away from home and your family. So many times, you have to put your trust in strangers. You have been so kind. I am sure you will do the right thing."

And with that, she squeezed my hand gently. I handed her a napkin and she wiped away her tears.

I paid the bill and we walked out of the restaurant. I felt her arm around my waist as she pulled me close to her as we walked back to my place. We sat sipping Calvados Coquerel.

"This is very nice. I have never had this before." She raised her glass and our glasses 'clinked'.

"Did you know it takes thirteen pounds of apples to make one 750 Millilitre bottle of this? That's what gives it the flavour of green apples, mint and a slightly floral finish."

"Bob, you know so many things. Did you study wines?"

"Not really. I've just read it on the label."

We laughed as we made our way to my bedroom.

It was seven o'clock the following morning when I was wakened by the ringing of my phone.

"Morning, Bob MacInally."

"Bob, I am in a phone box. Did you see the television last night? I think you call the programme Watch crime."

"Crimewatch?"

"Yes, Crimewatch. The lady said that a lady's head had been found and an artist had made painting of the lady's face. I tell you I just about die, I say oh my God it is Nadya. I go to shop and buy newspaper her face is in paper. She not have smile very straight, no, how you say expression. What should I do? The paper say 'do you know this woman?' and then it say tell the Police, what I do if I tell Police I could be next."

"Vesta, don't do anything and most of all don't let the Russian see the paper. I will deal with it. I will speak to you later."

Elensa looked at me. She held out her arms and walked towards me. She put her arms around my neck and pulled me close to her.

"Bob, what is wrong? Was it a bad phone call?"

"Yes, a very bad phone call. One of the girls I have been looking for, I think she has been murdered."

Chapter 27
Let's Have a Listen

House in Dummer

Vesta sat talking with me. I could not tell her the full story. I had to lie to her over certain details. I could not tell her or anyone else for that matter the full story. Anyway, who would believe it? When Vesta left, I sat wondering what to do next. Deep down, I felt sure the house at Dummer was the crime scene, a hunch? Detectives were not allowed to have such a thing. That was old fashioned and not allowed in today's politically correct society. Any evidence that was available was circumstantial perhaps I should have left the bags with the clothing at the collection point but then again I had saved what I believed was Nadya's clothing. I walked through to my kitchen and was putting on the kettle when I noticed Liz's card with The Salvation Army flag on the front in my letter rack. I removed it from the rack and read the back where Liz had written Psalm 72-Verses 12–14. Just what did that mean? I hadn't a clue. I made a cup of coffee and walked into my living room and searched along my bookshelf and found my grandfather's well used Bible. I opened it and looked through the Psalms, the last time I had opened or read a Bible was at Sunday school when I was about twelve years old. I found Psalm 72, Verses 12–14. It read:

12 For he shall deliver the needy when he crieth; the poor also, and him that hath no helper.

13 He shall spare the poor and the needy, and shall save the souls of the needy.

14 He shall redeem their soul from deceit and violence: and precious shall their blood be in his sight.

I read these verses over and over again. I suppose I would call myself Christian, but not a 'Holly Wullie' as they would say in Scotland. This passage had been given to me by someone whose life I had seen changed in the short time I had known her.

I sat down with my cup of tea, the words I had read kept going through my mind, 'and him that hath no helper'. Those kids had no helper when they were crying out for help. Well, who knows perhaps I can do something? I picked up my telephone and dialled the Chelsea number and then sent an electronic signal down the line. After a few seconds, I could hear what was going on in the flat. There was no sound until after about ten minutes when I heard a door open and then close again, and someone entered the room. It sounded like Vesta as she talked to herself in her own language. It was almost as if she was praying. There were all the usual sounds from within the house. After a short time, a door closed and a man spoke he had a strong Eastern European accent, which was more pronounced as he shouted.

"Bitch, are you here?"

"Yes, I am here in the kitchen." It was Vesta.

"Come here. I want you."

I could hear her voice getting louder as she came into the room.

"Yes, I was washing dishes."

"Well, stop now and you fuck off for two hours. I have got business to do."

"Yes, I will get my jacket."

"Don't piss me about get your jacket now and get out of here."

"Okay I go now."

"Piss off."

I heard the door close as she left. The man mumbled to himself as he walked around the room. He then picked up the handset of the phone and I switched on the recorder. A number was dialled and after a short spell, a female answered.

"Hello."

"Megan?"

"Yes."

"It's me, Sergei, can you talk?"

"Yes, okay."

"Have you seen the newspaper today?"

"No, what is it?"

"The bitch who was giving us the problem, she is in the papers today."

"Hold on I have a paper in the kitchen, one minute."

"Oh my God it's her, the bitch Nadya."

"Yes, you are correct, Megan. It is her. I said bury the head a long way from the house, so what did you do with it?"

"Put in with the rubbish from the house; it must have fallen out some place. What did you do with her other bits?"

"Don't worry about them. They are a long way from the house. Dogs and foxes will have taken care of them. That was months ago. They are well gone. Did you burn all her clothes as I told you?"

"Yes, yes they have all gone."

"And the tools?"

"I put them in skip outside a house in Basildon."

"Good, now you tell me did you put lots of the bleach chemical in the bath and down drain, yes?"

"Yes, I washed it so many times. There was so much blood."

"That is good, and the passports?"

"I think I gave you all the passports, was hers with them, yes?"

"Yes, you took them and said you would put them safe."

"Yes, I have put them safe and I am the only one with a key."

"You sure?"

"Yes, sure, I keep the key very safe and away from the embassy."

"That's good, that Ameer has given us so much trouble he didn't have to do what he did. Do you think he gets his kicks from killing?"

"Who knows? The person I worry about is the other bitch Tet, 'um, whatever her name is."

"Tetyana?"

"Yes, that is her, I do not think she will be near us. She knows what is coming to her if she comes near me. I have the very place for her, head or no head."

"How long do you think we will have to keep Ameer happy?"

"I am not sure the top man at the embassy appears happy. It's all to do with some deal they are working on. I don't know too much but he seems happy that we have got Ameer, how you say? Hooked?"

"Yes, hooked. Has there been any problems from the people who lost the gold?"

"No, the police still think it was stolen by a rival gang who had stolen it from the airport and I don't think for one minute that gang is going to walk into a police station and say someone has stolen our gold."

This was followed by laughter on both sides and then the call was terminated.

I played the recording over and over again.

"What did you do with her other bits?"

My blood ran cold.

"Don't worry about them. They are a long way from the house. The dogs and foxes will have taken care of them. That was months ago they are well gone."

My mind went back to a couple of months before. The man in the cemetery, Wullie eh? The Scottish guy with his wee Skye Terrier, Wullie McIntyre 'Shug' it had a forearm – bone in its mouth as it came out of the bushes. Was this a part of Nadya? A kid who had left her home full of hope only to be raped and murdered by these people?

I made up my mind to fix these people once and for all.

Chapter 28
The Last Straw

I don't know whether it was the result of their phone conversation or the press reports of all the villains, child abusers and all the 'no goods' of this country walking out of courts and sticking two fingers up as they left as free men due to some technicality, which their solicitors had found in the case. What the hell had an error in some cop's notebook got to do with justice? The anger was boiling up inside me something I had never felt whilst a serving officer, our attitude had always been 'they will come again'. Many did but not before they had ruined the lives of many innocent people. I felt I was going through a frightening stage. I so wanted to teach them a lesson they would never forget.

Over the next few weeks, I listened in to the flat at Chelsea. There was nothing of any significance until I received a call from Vesta to tell me that the next evening, Sergio would be coming to the flat.

The following evening, somewhere around six o'clock, I activated the listening device at the Chelsea flat. There were the usual domestic sounds, dishes being stored with some music playing in the background. At five to seven, I switched on my recorder. At seven o'clock, I heard a door open and the then close.

"Hello, my little bitch, where are you?"

It was Sergio.

"Bitch, where are you?"

Vesta answered.

"Never mind the coffee. I have some presents for you."

"Presents?"

"Yes, here open the bag, catch."

There was thud as the bag hit the floor followed by a rustling sound as the bag was picked up and opened.

"I do not wear underwear like this."

Vesta's voice trembled.

"You do tonight you little---"

He said something in Russian.

"What do you think I am? I am not your slave."

"Oh, yes you are and don't forget your dear little brother at home; I know a nice big Russian man who would like him. Perhaps he would like him as his slave and who knows your brother might like it. How would you like a little gay brother?"

There was the sound of Vesta being slapped.

"Now, strip and put your gift on."

He continued speaking in Russian as Vesta sobbed and pleaded in her native tongue for the man to stop.

It was to no avail as he dragged her into another room.

I wanted to drive to London to try and save her but I was too far away and would never have made it in time and anyway, I would have ended up killing him and that was for another day.

I was helpless, walking away from the telephone I found myself punching the armchair. Shaking with anger, I let my tape recorder do the rest.

Chapter 29
Time to Put the Cat Amongst the Pigeons

The telephone rang and broke the silence and brought me down to earth.

"Hi, Bob, it's Liz. Thought I would give you a ring to see how you are doing, you have been in my thoughts over the past few days. I kept saying to myself I must ring Bob, so here I am, you okay?"

"Yeah, I'm fine doing a little bit of work but nothing too exciting and yourself?"

"I'm busy doing work with the 'old Army'. I'm helping out at a hostel and refuge for girls who were doing 'the business' and for a hundred and one reasons have given it up, drugs, booze and S.T.Ds. I had been told a few years ago that girls from foreign countries were being brought over here to be put on the game I would not have believed it. It's an industry worth millions of pounds to the gangs who are running it. Lots come from the Far East but the majority are from the Eastern Bloc. The government doesn't seem to be doing anything about it. We do our best but as usual, there is not enough money. We run charity events to help, many prayers are said and I'm sure some day one will work. After all, Major Mary's worked for me. Oh, by the way, did you have any joy in tracing the girl from Mallorca?"

"Yes, she was found, not by me but she too is in hiding from the people who brought her over from her country on a 'con' and put her on the game. It's a long story but I am sure these people will get their just desserts one day, or will they?"

"Well, Bob, we must trust in the Lord, and I'll bet you never thought you would have heard me say that in Puerto Pollenca. But I can assure you it has worked for me."

"It certainly seems to have worked for you. I have seen a big change in you, Liz."

"Thanks, Bob, it can work for anyone. There I go sounding like a preacher. I am proud to say it worked for me a drunk and a 'prozzi' off the streets of Liverpool."

"No, I don't think you are preaching. Keep up the good work and keep in touch."

"Okay, Bob speak later."

With that, she hung up.

I sat staring at the phone. Twenty minutes earlier I had listened to girl being raped followed by a young woman whose life had been turned around and now she is helping others. What a mixed-up world we live in.

I switched on the tape and listened. There was no doubt in my mind that Vesta had been subjected to a terrible ordeal. She didn't scream, her sobbing said it all. Whilst she sobbed, he ranted on in Russian laughing between each sentence. On completion of his attack, his voice got louder as he returned to the room.

"Get up and get your clothes on, bitch. I want you out of here in thirty minutes."

Vesta's crying slowly stopped. After a while, she came back into the room.

"Go and wash your face and wipe the makeup from your face you look like a circus clown, the time is coming for you to meet Mister Stanley."

I could hear water running and after a short time, Vesta returned into the room.

"There you are, that's better. So give me a kiss and go out. Come back in two hours."

The door of the flat closed leaving Sergio singing to himself.

Pressing the 'eject' button, the tape popped out of the D.A.T. recorder. Slowly removing and installing a new tape, I switched the tape to record and at the same time switched on the listening device.

Closing the front door behind me, I walked to the Lord Raglan public house and ordered a pint of beer and sat down to read my newspaper.

"Hi, Bob."

It was old Tom; he made his way over to me with the aid of two crutches.

"How's it going, Tom?"

"Yeah, okay the legs are still playing me up."

I had never asked him what had caused his physical condition.

"Are you still okay to give me a lift to Heathrow next week?"

"Yes, no problem, just give me the flight time and I'll get you there. Where are you off to this time?"

"Vegas, I'm staying at the Luxor Hotel on the south end of the strip."

"You have been there before, was that last year?"

"Two years ago and I'll be meeting up with the lady I met then. I don't know if you remember her?"

"Was that the lovely Cheryl?"

"The very one. By the way, I've got myself a new electric wheelchair; it's a beauty. They tell me it has got a range of about fifty miles on one charge of the battery and it is suitable for rough terrain so it will be ideal when I go fishing. I got a new van with side windows to carry it. It makes life so much easier; it's got ramps that come out the back on the push of a button and then I can drive in and scramble into the driving seat, push a button the ramps slide back in and the back doors close automatically. You can use it to take me up to the airport next week and use it for your work. Nobody would 'sus' you then."

We finished our drinks and after the usual putting the world to rights, we went our separate ways.

I arrived home, poured myself a drink and sat down to listen to the tape recording. The sound of drinks being poured was the first thing on the tape. There was then a conversation about gold and it appeared that Sergio had been storing it for the person in the room. He had been trusted him with a previous load and had been paid about a million United States Dollars for doing so with the promise of the same amount on delivery of the second load. There had to be a tremendous amount of trust here or was a threat hanging over Sergio. What would let these people trust a man with all this gold and how did they get hold of it? From what I picked up from the tape, they were planning a meeting in a few days' time in the Hilton Hotel in Trader Vic's bar in London. The deal was to be as before. The gold would be in a van parked in a nearby car park, it would be as the last time hidden in specially adapted fire extinguishers. The van would have 'fire and safety' on the sides and rear. The plan had been well worked out and had obviously been successful on the previous hand over. Sergio convinced the man that he was the only one who knew where the store was and that was going to remain as it was. But how would he transport it from the tomb?

There would be a difference this time. There would be no gold. I was going to relieve them of it.

The following day, I bought two handheld 'walkie talkie radios' from one of the Indian run shops in Tottenham Court Road in London. It was important that they did not have a good transmitting range and were battery operated, not rechargeable. I paid in cash and likewise at the garage where I purchased the batteries to fit.

I was sitting at home wearing my surgical gloves fitting the batteries into the radios.

The telephone rang; it was Vesta. She was in a coin box in the Kings Road in Chelsea.

"Hi, Bob, just a quick call to let you know Sergio will be out of the country for five days he leaves tomorrow. I think he is going to Russia. He spoke with a man this morning and tell him, he says it is business."

If I were going to have that gold, I would have to have it whilst he was away. I could not ask anyone to assist me. I already had a plan in my head but I had to be able to keep observation in the cemetery. Not an easy task.

I went into a local stonemason and explained I had a couple of old family headstones to clean. The stonemason was very helpful and sold me a liquid to spray on the stones and explained that all the dirt and moss would come off in a short time. If the letters are in raised lead, get yourself a cork and wrap a piece of rag around it and then put the cork and rag gently into some paint and touch the raised letters and they will come up like new. (That was how I cleaned two gravestones as I kept observation for a few days as I waited for the Russian to arrive.)

I returned to the cemetery the following day and searched for an area close to the tomb where I could hide the gold under the cover of darkness. I eventually found a place nearby, it was in the middle of some graves and set off the pathway some ten feet. It looked as if some months before someone had pruned trees and left the branches to rot. On top of this, various dead flowers and wreaths had been discarded. I took hold of the main branch and lifted it; it came up like a large piecrust revealing a hollow beneath it. I had found the hiding place for MY gold. I left the area and went and had a meal near Waterloo Bridge.

It was misty when I returned some hours later. There was a heavy dampness on the trees making the place even more eerie as the heavy drops of water fell from the branches onto the undergrowth scaring the wits out of me. I hid in the bushes till gone midnight. It was now or never, shit or bust. On went my gloves as I crossed the pathway. Slipping the key from the pocket of my Barbour jacket,

I pulled the straps on my rucksack tighter and shone the beam from my torch towards the metal door as I made my way down the stairs. I fell back as a black cat jumped over me. I cursed it without thinking as my yell seemed to waken the dead in this most unholy place.

I shook as I stood shivering in silence. After what seemed an eternity, I put the key into the lock and gently turned it. The bolt shot back and I was in, gently pushing the door closed behind I made my way down towards the corpses and the gold. I started to load the bars into my rucksack. I felt really scared as the reality of what I was doing registered with me. I had been swept along on the tide of excitement. I tried to pick up my bag but it was far too heavy, it had to be emptied of some of the ingots. This meant more time wasted. Picking up the bag, I struggled up the staircase and across the road and emptied the ingots into their hiding place. It was only when I returned to the staircase I found the door open. Had I left it like that or was some person inside?

I switched off my torch and listened for any sound from within. The only sound came from the wind whistling down the stairs and into the tomb, the first to have reached the inside of the tomb since the Braithwaites were laid to rest.

Slowly, I walked down the stairs in total darkness as I reached the bottom I stood motionless my heart pounding. Switching on the torch, I swept the inside of the tomb with the beam.

An elongated screech sounded out as a bloody cat ran past me. Falling to my knees, I dropped onto the bottom step. I honestly thought I was having a heart attack. After what seemed an eternity, I stood up and walked in and started to fill my rucksack with more ingots. I don't know many journeys back and forward I made pulling the door behind me on each occasion. I could not face another encounter with that bloody devil cat.

Returning for a final check of the tomb, I looked around and in the corner was a large briefcase similar to the type used by aircrew. Both combination locks were locked. I picked it up and started to carry it upstairs and then I remembered the Ozi and the passports, it was another quick trip down stairs to collect them, soon they were along with the gold and the briefcase. Only one more visit left. I picked up my plastic Tesco shopping bag and returned downstairs. Opening the bag, I removed one of the 'walkie-talkies' and placed it and some extra batteries next to the car batteries. Next to that, I left a type written note on A4 size paper. I climbed back up the stairs, locked the door and scattered a few leaves around the bottom. I did a double check and made sure everything looked undisturbed.

Collecting the briefcase, I walked back to my car. It was the first time I was aware of the weight it was heavy, the thought ran through my mind, was it more body parts?

I was so glad to reach home, shower and crash into bed and into a sound sleep. What was I turning myself into? A grave-robber? A thief? A murderer?

Chapter 30
Disabled?

The phone rang wakening me from my sound sleep, I looked at my watch it was 10 a.m.

"Morning, Bob, Tom here. How you doing, my old son?"

"Yeah, fine."

"You sound pissed, were you at it last night?"

"No, working."

"I suppose she's lying next to you."

"No, honestly, I was grafting all night."

"Yes, that's what I meant. The reason I phoned was to see if you are still okay to take me to Heathrow tomorrow. My flight is at ten in the morning so I'll have to be there at about seven thirty, is that okay?"

"No problem. I'll be at your 'drum' about six, okay?"

"Fine and use my car, you can get right up to the door with my disabled badge."

"See you then, cheers."

As I started to prepare my coffee, I remembered the briefcase and the passports in the boot of car. I walked outside and collected them. Once indoors, I started to work out the combination numbers.

What was I going to do?

Give the case back to him?

The next day was an early start to collect Tom for his airport run. The whole conversation was taken up with Tom telling me about his new 'toy', how it could climb bloody mountains and carry tons, my ears pricked up on the 'carry tons' part.

I dropped him off at the airport and made my way to South London and the cemetery. I parked inside the gates and manoeuvred the invalid scooter out of the back of his van. Locking all the van doors, I climbed onto the seat of his four-wheeled invalid chair. I switched on the ignition key and the handle bar consul lit up like a Christmas tree. Pulling on a little lever, the scooter slowly moved forward increasing speed as I put more pressure on the lever.

Making my way along the gravel paths, I found the vehicle very easy to handle. After a few circuits around the gold stash making sure there was no one in the vicinity and making sure the stash had not been disturbed, I stopped and got off and walked over to the compost heap and gently lifted the branch exposing the gold which glistened in the sunlight. Picking up one ingot, I placed it in the wire basket on the front of the scooter. I reckoned the basket could carry at least another eight. I loaded them in and covered them with my waterproof jacket. I filled the rear basket and covered it with more of Tom's clothing.

I gave the scooter a trial run with the gold. Tom was correct it did feel as if it could carry a ton. I managed to offload the gold into the van with no difficulty and returned on a number of occasions each time carrying the load in the front and rear baskets. During the moving of the gold, I never saw one person I could not believe my luck, particularly when moving the Ozi wrapped in my jacket. This had to be removed from the tomb. I had plans for it and besides I did not want the Russian using it. Soon the chair was loaded onto the van and I was on my way home praying there would be no mishaps on the journey.

My car was parked outside Tom's house. After driving it away from the front of his garage doors, I drove his van up onto his driveway and into his garage locking the door behind me. I then reversed my car up to the doors and walked home stopping at the Lord Raglan public house for a well-deserved pint or two.

On my arrival at home, there was a voice message from Vesta saying she would call me the following morning at ten.

Perhaps it was the two beers or the exertion of moving gold (how bad was that) but I was soon fast asleep in my armchair, legs stiff and cold and wondering to myself why I hadn't gone to bed when I came home instead of sitting down for five minutes. It seemed as if I had just sat down when I wakened and looked at my watch. Seven thirty, time to move the gold.

I had some breakfast and walked to Tom's house with everything racing through my mind. What if his house had been screwed and the gold nicked or even worse if the thieves had been found in the house with the gold? Tom would have a lot of explaining to do and what about my car being on his drive.

I did not have long to wait, everything was fine. I climbed into my car and moved it forward on the drive. Why do nosey neighbours always stick their noses in when they are least wanted?

"Good morning, did Tom get away okay yesterday?"

It was the next-door neighbour.

"He's fine all in good time, no problems."

"I saw the car outside last night and I thought that's strange what with Tom being away, you know or perhaps you don't. I'm involved in neighbourhood watch, oh I am Nancy by the way."

I thought to myself, *Nosey bugger, this is all I need.*

"I phoned my contact at the local police station and surprise, he was there. I immediately reported the suspect car to him he and came straight down, well I say straight, it was two hours later. Mind you I suppose these chaps have so much to do."

"Yes, it never stops for them."

"It's amazing he told me not to worry as he knew who the car belonged to."

"Amazing."

"And then I thought I wonder if it's Tom's friend the policeman and here you are."

"Yes, here I am. I thought I would put his chair batteries on charge and get some of my heavy shopping out of his van and into my car."

"Let me get my Rod to help you."

She looked over her shoulder and called into the house.

"Rod, come out and give, I'm sorry I didn't get your name."

"Bob, but honestly it's okay I can manage."

Rod appeared at the front door complete with his tweed coat and cap and car keys in his hand.

"Are you ready dear, time to leave for Diana's, she will be waiting."

"Oh sorry, Bob. I had completely forgotten about our date with our daughter over in Pangbourne, sorry must rush, bye-bye."

I mumbled to myself 'thank God for Diana', all I would have needed is that nosey old cow discovering the gold.

Within two minutes, they were in their car and driving off and waving a 'royal goodbye'.

Pangbourne, by the time they get there and back, have their meal that should give me at least three hours to load my car and leave.

I loaded the car, drove back home and put my car in the garage and locked up. I was feeling very tired, and immediately fell asleep on the chair. After a couple of hours, I wakened with a jolt and was immediately wide awake.

I had left the Ozi under the wheel chair in Tom's car. I broke into a cold sweat, the phone rang, it was Vesta.

"Bob, it's Vesta, you okay?"

"Yes, I am fine, and you?"

"Yes, good I am in a phone box. The Russian pig is coming back to London tomorrow. He says he has left his flat keys in the flat and wants me to be at the flat at two p.m. as he wants to get in to collect something. I can only guess it will be that key. Did you ever find out what it was for?"

"No, I never did."

I hated lying to her, but what I was planning could only be kept to myself.

"I have to go now. That's the gas man at the door. I have a problem with my central heating. Call me back if you have any more news, bye."

More lies to this lovely girl.

I walked to Tom's house and successfully loaded the Ozi into my holdall and walked home with a cold sweat running down the small of my back. Some things can be excused if stopped by police, but an Ozi complete with a suppresser and ammunition. I don't think so.

Arriving home, I flopped into my armchair and tried to get my wits about me. Sitting next to the armchair was the airline bag. I needed to get the combination to open the case. I don't think so. Let's get a screwdriver, that'll do the trick.

Pop, pop and it opened. I folded the two covers open. I could not believe my eyes the case was filled with hundreds of US dollar bills, most seemed to be at least in denominations of one hundred US dollars. There was a lot of money here, plus the gold, it made my pension look rather silly. Then I remembered the drugs, Sergio can have them he may well need them.

Opening the plastic shopping bag, I discovered fourteen foreign passports. All were for females aged between nineteen years and twenty-two. Amongst them was one for Nadya Davidovich, the name on the correspondence amongst the rubbish from Dummer. Her innocent child like face stared at me. She had beautiful Jewish features. The thought went through my mind 'what had her family gone through during the war for their grandchild to be killed and hacked to pieces in England so many years later'? After a further search, there was

Tetyana. As I opened it at the photo section, her smiling face looked up at me. Little did she know what was facing her when she posed for this picture.

The rest of the day was spent working out the next move but first I had to count the money. This took most of the morning and by reckoning, I made it to be somewhere in excess of seven hundred thousand US dollars. I showered, got changed and made my way to Wokingham and Barclay's Bank where I opened a large safety deposit box and deposited the dollars. I then made my way to Bracknell Council tip where I ripped the case apart and threw it onto the mountain of household waste. I knew I only had a couple of days left before Sergio returned to the UK and I wanted to be in a position to complete my plan as soon as he returned to the cemetery.

Chapter 31
Too Late to Turn Back

The things that puzzled me were, how was he going to get the gold out of the vault on his own? Why was he using an old Ford and not a Diplomatic car with all the benefits, anyway at this stage, that should not affect me.

I drove down to South London, collected some sandwiches and newspapers on the way and parked up near the cemetery gates and waited in the hope that the Russian would arrive on his own. Hours passed by and my eyelids were closing longer than they were supposed to. I was fighting off sleep. I could feel my head dropping and with a jolt, I was sitting upright. Had I been sleeping for a few seconds or an hour? It had always been a problem when doing observations on your own, particularly when waiting for someone or something to arrive. Then the thought of the need for a pee arose, peeing into a plastic bag is not the easiest thing to do whilst sitting in the front seat of a car. Years of practice and I had almost perfected it, unfortunately spillages did occur.

True to form, the Ford drove past and parked when I was in mid-stream. The Russian got out of the car and walked through the cemetery gates. I managed to stop peeing, tied the top of the plastic bag and got out of the car zipping up my trouser fly as I did so. Shutting the car door quietly, I followed 'my man' along the pathway. I was about one hundred yards behind him. Stopping at one of the few attended graves I picked up a bunch of flowers from the top of the grave and carried on following him. I was surprised he never once looked over his shoulder. I suppose he had walked this route so many times without incident that it had become second nature to him. When he was approaching the path to 'Walters house', I knelt down at a grave and placed the flowers at the headstone. Remaining in the same position, I could see he was now some one hundred and fifty yards ahead of me. He stopped and looked to his left and right and then vanished into the bushes. Getting up, I walked quickly to the point where I had last seen him. My stomach was churning. It was now or never. The silence was broken by a well familiar sound to me, the sound of the tomb door opening. The silence resumed and was then broken by the sound of the door closing. I looked over the stonework at the side of the staircase the door was being closed from the inside. I looked down. Sergio looked up and stared through the gap at the side of the door. He was staring straight at me. He pulled the door closed and then apparently thought better of it and started to push it open, as he did so I vaulted down onto the bottom of the staircase and slammed against the door trying to close it. The door key fell from my pocket as I struggled to close the door fully and pick up the key at the same time. There was no resistance from inside. I guessed he must have fallen down the stairs.

Fumbling, I got my key into the keyhole and turned it, locking him inside. I pushed leaves back into position followed by more rubble and tree stumps, as I left I looked back, content with my work, the bottom of the staircase looked as if no one had been there for years and most of all the door could not be pushed open from the inside.

He was secure in his soundproof room and whether I liked it or not my plan had now started to take place.

I walked away from the tomb and made my way back to my car replacing the flowers on the original grave as I did so.

I made my way to a local fish and chip shop where I had my supper. After darkness fell, it was back to where the Ford Motor car was parked. I stood next to the near-side passenger door and tried to open it. It was locked, there was only one thing for it, a large stone left my hand and smashed the nearside window, continuing walking I returned to my car and waited. After about an hour, I drove past where the Ford had been, only broken glass remained.

Guessing the local youths had seen my invitation to go 'joy riding' my plan was falling into place. There was no doubt the car would be abandoned miles from the area where it was stolen and possibly burnt out.

Chapter 32
A Good Night's Sleep

As my head hit the pillow, I fell sound asleep until seven o'clock the following morning. On wakening, it felt as if the events of the previous day had all been a dream, gradually reality kicked in. I had Sergio where I wanted him and by now, I guess he would have found my instructions together with the radio and batteries, that's assuming he had not killed himself falling down the stairs.

Making my way to the area near the cemetery, I parked the car, put the other radio in my pocket and walked to a bench near Stanley's house, sitting down I switched the radio on. Sergio's written instructions were to switch his on at twelve noon.

Looking at my watch, it was showing one minute to noon. The hand moved five, four, three, two, one.

Twelve noon.

"Hello, my little Russian friend, are you receiving?" Silence, and then his radio crackled.

"Who the hell are you?"

"That does not matter. I know who you are. Can I take it you have read my instructions?"

"To hell with you, open this door now or you are a dead man."

"I do not think so, we both have keys, the big difference is you do not have a keyhole."

"When the people find out you have their gold they will kill you for sure."

"Gold, what are you talking about?"

"I think you know. I ask again who are you and what do you want, open the door and I will see if I can help."

"You will know by now your mobile telephone does not operate under ground, so you are on your own and I hold all the cards, so stop your crap and listen to me."

"You are either an idiot or a very brave man."

"I am neither, have you read my letter?"

"Yes, but I have no idea who you think I am. What is this rubbish about Nadya, Noleen and someone called Ameer? I have never heard of such people."

"I can assure you by this time tomorrow when you want some food, water and you will be living with your own piss and shit you will start to remember."

"Do not forget yesterday I saw your face and I will remember it."

"Good, and by the way, your nice little car has gone. So, until tomorrow at two p.m., I will say good bye."

"No, wait."

With that, I switched off the radio and left the cemetery. On my return home, I telephoned Elensa and arranged to pick her up at her flat and go for a meal at Rossini's.

Once again, the meal was up to Toni's high standard. The more I was enjoying her company, the more I kept thinking of Sergio, hungry, thirsty and no doubt cold in the tomb. I immediately turned my thoughts to the tape recording, the rape and the disposing of that poor girl's body. The world was a safer place with that Russian rat in his rat hole.

"Bob, you okay?"

It was Elensa.

"You were in another world, Bob, you thinking about work?"

"Yes, a little bit, but not let's not talk about that. Now is the time to think about this moment and let tomorrow take care of itself."

We sat sipping our wine and staring at each other. Slowly her hand reached over the table and held mine; after having finished the wine and settling the bill, we left the restaurant and walked back to Vesta's flat. She had seen a difference in me.

"Bob, you are worrying about something, is it me?"

"No, it is nothing like that."

"So you are worried about something, you want to leave me, yes?"

"No, no let me tell you. Do you go to church?"

"I am a Catholic and we as children were made to go. I kept going until I came here. Why do you ask?"

"A lady gave me a card with some words on it. Hold on a minute, I have it in my jacket pocket." I reached in and took it from my pocket and handed it to her. She looked at it and read out 'Psalm seventy, Verses twelve to fourteen'.

"What does it mean? One minute and I will find out."

She left the room and after a few minutes returned carrying a small Bible and pink rosary beads.

"This is the Bible and rosary beads I was given at my first Communion. Show me again the part from the Bible."

She took the card from me and searched through the Bible looking for the passage.

"Ah, here it is. I think the translation means, God will help people who have no people to help them, it then talks about deceit and violence and their blood is, how you say, important. Perhaps it would be better if a Father explained it. I am not very good at these things. Maybe it is what they would read to soldiers going to war? You know going to help innocent people."

It did not help very much. I should have spent more time in Sunday School. After another two hours at Vesta's, I made my way home. I had an early start the following morning.

Chapter 33
The Russian Wants to Do a Deal

It was a bright summer's day as I entered the cemetery and sat down on the bench and fitted the earpiece from my radio. I spread out my sandwich wrapper on the bench next to me. Connecting the small microphone to the radio. I switched it on and listened. Sergio had his handset switched on.

"Hello, hello." Silence.

"Hello, hello."

"Ah, good morning, little Russian man. How are you this beautiful morning, sleep well?"

"Okay, cut the crap and let's do a deal."

"Once again, let me remind you I hold all the aces."

"Fine, tell me what you want. You can keep the gold. I have got to get out of here I have things to do."

"Let's face facts. You are going to be sharing that room with the Stanley's for some time so don't waste your energy telling me what to do, understand?"

"What do you want?"

"Firstly, put the pocket watch back in the coffin where it belongs, and do it now."

There was then a pause.

"You know too much for your own good. When I get out of here, you better vanish."

"Stop right there, I am the person who decides when you get out, if ever."

"Where are my dollars?"

"They will be put to good use. The more I think of you and your friends, the more I despise you people."

"What people?"

"You people who come to my country, bring innocent young women here, drug them and then put them on the game, rape them, kill them and then throw their bodies out like rubbish."

"I do not know what you are talking about."

"Don't lie or I will bring Megan to join you."

"Do you think I will stay still in here when you try to put her in this hole? You are a fool."

"Do you think you will have the strength to do that in two weeks' time, now who is the fool."

"GRYANZNYI PODONOK."

"Now, now keep a civil tongue in your head. It puts me off my sandwich and coffee to hear you talk like that. What does it mean?"

"Evil bastard."

His voice was getting hoarse; it was obvious he was in need of water.

"I will have to leave you now I have things to do, and so have you. I want you to tell me where Ameer's ship will be in the next few weeks. I will contact you at twelve noon in the next couple of days, so don't be wasting your battery power by leaving the radio switched on."

"You can't do this to me."

"Yes, I can and please remember I am a man of my word and that is more than you were when you brought poor little Nadya from her homeland. And you call me an evil bastard?"

"Just one minute I can help you if—"

I had enough talking and switched off my radio to give him a couple of days to reflect, besides I had other things to do and he was only my first target.

Returning to Dummer, I parked my car a few miles from the manor and made my way across the fields and entered the woods that surrounded the grounds of the house. Finding a point where I could hopefully see which car was being used by Megan, I remained hidden in the woods at a point where I had a clear view of the front of the manor. There was no movement to or from the house; neither were any of the cars I had seen previously present. It was not until seven o'clock when the luxury minibus arrived driven by a woman. She parked the vehicle away from the house, got out and shut the driver's door, walked from the vehicle giving the bonnet a gentle pat as if she was leaving a horse after a period of riding. She walked up the staircase and entered the house. The lights came on inside giving the impression that she was at home on her own. After an hour, I crept through the woods until I was close to the minibus. Coming out of the woods, I slowly made my way to the rear of the vehicle, my heart pounding as I reached the rear. Gently reaching for the boot handle, I turned it; it was unlocked after closing it gently. The alarm had not been activated.

I returned to the woods and eventually to my car and home. On the journey, I remembered there had been a conversation about bringing another six girls over to supply to the Arab at his boat. This was going to my chance to sort out Megan.

At home, I found Nadya's passport and deposited it in one of the two rubbish bags next to her clothing. The other passports were left in the original shopping bag and these too were put into one of the plastic bags from the manor house. I also removed and destroyed the petrol receipts from South London. In the other bag, I deposited the Ozi and ammunition; it was now time for a trip to Dummer and return the bags to their owner.

The journey with my 'dangerous' load to say the least was scary. Finding what I thought would be a suitable place to park I pulled into a 'lovers car park' backing onto some woods. After a few minutes, I got out of the car, looked about and opened the boot of the car and removed the bags and quietly closed the boot lid. Next, it was through the woods, across fields and after what seemed an age, I reached the single-track road outside the gates of Braithwaite Manor where the bags had been deposited some months before.

Stretching over the wire fence, I lifted one bag over followed by the other and rested them at the top of the ditch. Panting, I climbed over the fence and slid down into the dry ditch. I reached up and pulled the bags next to me. After a few minutes of getting my breath back, I climbed out and lay in the long grass listening for any noise. Apart from the sound of the occasional cow mooing and chewing the cud, the night air was ghostly still. Pulling the bags up to me, I lay still for a few more minutes.

Raising my head above the long grass, I looked left and right; no car headlights; no late-night walkers. It was now or never. Grabbing hold of the bags I stood up and ran across the road and fell into the ditch on the opposite side of the road the bags tumbling next to me, I kept thinking, 'I'm too old for this game'. There was nothing else for it but to 'plough on'. The bags were getting heavier as I reached the edge of the woods close to the Mini bus. Waiting for some ten minutes, I was convinced there was nobody in the vicinity. All I had to hope for now was that the boot of the bus was still unlocked and unalarmed.

I crept over and reached out to the handle, turned it and the boot opened assisted by the hydraulics; it was time to load the boot with the bags, as they went in I ripped one open exposing the Ozi. Gently reaching up, I pulled the lid down inserting a piece of straw between the lid and the coachwork; turning the handle and the lid was secure.

It was now back to my car and home for a few hours' sleep.

Chapter 34
In Memory of Nadya

It was a chance I had to take, assuming she was going to Heathrow Airport to collect the six girls that had been talked about there was a flight due in at eleven o'clock in the morning. Her route would be by the M3 Motorway and therefore she would pick it up at a nearby junction near Dummer. At eight a.m., I took up a position at the junction. An hour passed and just when I was thinking 'I had got it all wrong', the minibus made its way onto the motorway and towards Heathrow Airport. After another forty minutes, it pulled up onto the open-air car park at Terminal Five and stopped. The female driver got out. I was convinced it was Megan. She used the key fob to lock the vehicle. The hazard lights flashed. She walked off and into the airport terminal followed by myself. She was greeted by the two Russian men I had photographed at the manor some months before.

I went back to the minibus and checked the boot door. The straw was still in place suggesting it had not been opened.

Making my way to a public telephone, I pulled my baseball cap down and held my mobile phone close to my face, a tactic used by all thieves to avoid being seen on CCTV.

Picking up the public phone, I dialled 999. The operator answered,

"Police, Fire or Ambulance which service do you require?"

"Police please."

"I am connecting you to a police operator now; what is your name, sir?"

"Peter Robinson."

"You are through to the police operator now."

"Police operator, how can I help?"

"I am at the car park at Terminal five at Heathrow, it is the open-air part. There is a minibus I have just seen a woman with a red coat and two men both with black leather jackets; they were at the boot and when they looked in, I saw what looked like a machine gun in the boot."

"A machine gun, what does it look like?"

"Black with a short barrel and a handle."

"What is your full name and address, sir?"

"I don't want to get involved. I am only trying to help. It's a dark-blue mini bus." I then gave him the registration number and replaced the handset.

I walked back to my car, changed my jacket and sat in the driver's seat. After about two minutes, two police officers arrived each carrying a sub-machine gun. They went straight to the minibus and started trying to look into the darkened windows. One of the officers was on his radio and writing in a notebook which he then showed to his colleague both shrugged their shoulders and walked away from the minibus and stood about twenty feet away looking over the parapet towards the terminal exit. Something obviously attracted their attention as they stood back from the parapet and one officer was speaking on his radio. They then moved further back from the parapet and stood between some parked cars.

After a few minutes, Megan and the two men arrived in company with six young women each pulling wheeled travel cases. The girls were laughing amongst themselves. As they approached the vehicle, two unarmed police officers appeared from the opposite side and stopped the three and appeared to ask for their passports, which were duly produced. One officer walked to the rear of the mini bus in company with Megan and took a bunch of keys from her. He then pressed the key fob and the hazard lights flashed and the doors unlocked. Megan lifted the boot lid and as she did so, the officer took hold of her arm and spun her around pinning her against the open boot lid when doing so he shouted 'firearm'. At that point, the two armed officers stepped forward guns pointing at the group. The two Russians put their arms in the air as they did so more armed officers arrived; weapons drawn and made the men lie on the ground, arms outstretched. In the meantime, Megan was handcuffed and held against the side of the minibus. Soon the area was swarming with police. The young girls were screaming and holding their heads. Two police vans arrived and a number of female officers scrambled out and went straight to the girls who were ushered into the vans and driven off. Two, what appeared plain clothes officers accompanied by a uniformed Inspector arrived and indicated to the officer holding Megan to bring her to the open boot of the vehicle. The inspector put on surgical gloves and reached into the boot and lifted out the Ozi holding it by the barrel. He showed it to Megan who shook her head from side to side. Next there followed the bag of passports; once again, the shake of the head. There was a conversation between the two of them as the Inspector picked up the hacksaw and the large knife; there was no head shaking this time, just the bowing of her head and a look of bewilderment as she screwed her face up. Placing the property back into the boot, the Inspector put his face close to hers and spoke. I guess he was cautioning her and telling her she was under arrest, she was led away by the officers. An officer who did not appear to be a 'ball of fire' had got hold of a roll of 'Police do not cross tape'. He looked as if he was counting his days to retirement as he sauntered around the car park tying the tape to anything he could find. Some things in the police never change. I drove out of the area with the feeling of a job well done.

As soon as I arrived home, I switched on the television news. The outside broadcast units had arrived and were already probing the scene with their telephoto lenses. Reporters were reporting 'reliable sources' had reported that nine suspects had been arrested and a mini bus containing an 'arsenal' of weapons had been recovered at the scene. The mini bus had been covered with a green plastic sheet and was being loaded onto a lorry.

The evening news covered the gates of the Manor House with a reporter holding a microphone and a notebook in her hand;

'The arrests of the suspected terrorists at Heathrow Airport this morning has taken an unusual twist with Police Forensic teams carrying out fingertip searches in Braithwaite Manor in the pretty post card village of Dummer here in Hampshire'.

Chapter 35
Two Down One More to Go

The following morning, papers were full of the stories one naming a Megan Owen from Wales as the woman arrested along with two Russians. There was no mention of the six girls.

It was time for me to make my way to South London and 'Stanley's house.' On reaching the cemetery, I took up my usual position on the bench and sat reading the newspapers as I waited for twelve noon; soon it arrived.

I looked about there was nobody around.

"Hello, Goldman."

Silence.

"Goldman, are you there?"

"Yes, yes."

His voice was very hoarse and he sounded as if he had a very dry throat.

"Ah, good morning, how are you?"

"I am not well, I need water and food, you must help, I am begging you, please."

"Yes, all in good time. Megan will not be coming to join you. I am afraid the police have got her and your two big Russian friends; hold on a minute, have you got time?"

"Yes of course you have, how silly of me, let me read to you todays Daily Mail newspaper."

I read through the headlines and the most important pieces.

"You still there?"

"Yes, I am still here; that has got nothing to do with me."

"Really, what about your fingerprints all over the passports, and I know at least one young lady who you raped, does the name Tetyana mean anything to you?"

"I can't speak. I am so thirsty."

"Okay, I am going to give a chance; you arranged for the six girls who were to go to Ameer's ship for that dirty scum to have as his slaves. What is the name of the ship and where is it?"

"I don't know."

"Yes, you do and you are going to tell me. I will be back in three days and I can guarantee you will tell me then, and if you do not, I will open the door and let the street boys in. I am sure you will remember them; these are ones who hit you after Tetyana ran away from you after you had brought her here to kill her. Now these boys will come in when I tell them how much heroin is in there. Understand?"

"I understand. Are you another police officer we can do deal with like your friends who told us where to get the gold from the airport?"

"Not exactly; I want Ameer's ship and where it is."

"Croesus and it will be in Palma Mallorca in two months' time."

"Thank you, now you listen and listen good; you gave Nadya to Ameer as if she was some sort of plaything, a toy, a packet of sweets for the packet to be discarded when he was finished with her. Well, when you and he were finished with her she was killed and you and that thing, Megan cut her to pieces. And what was your biggest problem? The innocent girl's blood, but you had the answer for that; use plenty of bleach, then between you, you disposed of her head in the local rubbish tip. Her parents don't even have her body to bury. Well, I can tell you now; neither will your family."

With that, I switched off my radio and left the cemetery with anger boiling within me.

Chapter 36
A 'Dirt Nap' for Sergio

I would have thought the furthest thing from Ameer's mind was the killing of Nadya and getting his two willing helpers to cut up the body and dispose of it. How many other girls had met the same fate, just wiped off the face of the earth never to be seen again and just for his so-called pleasure. It was, as I got older, becoming more convincing that there was no justice for people like him. They go through the system and frequently have the charges reduced and likewise their sentence. One guy caught bang to rights climbing out of an antique dealer's window with the stolen property. Two young cops who would not know what a fit up was took him to court where he pleaded 'guilty'. The newspapers told the story how he had seventy previous convictions for the same type of offence but the wise old judge gave him one hundred hours Community Service. That taught him a lesson he would never forget, and a good story he would tell to his mates down the pub that night.

"Bastard!"

The chance of getting enough evidence to arrest and convict Ameer was so slim that I doubt if the case would be followed up. Megan's story, if she decided to tell the truth, would not help and besides who would corroborate it? It would not be Sergio as it would be assumed that he would have long since gone back to Russia and the chances of finding him there were nil.

The newspapers and television carried on reporting the stories surrounding the Manor at Dummer. Neighbours were interviewed but could not add very much other than to say the people who visited the Manor 'kept themselves to themselves'. One woman from the local pub said she had seen the Welsh lady eating in the bar in company with three Russian men, two were large men and one was much smaller. The lady never spoke in Russian and frequently sat quietly as the other three had whispered conversations. There was nothing new. It was obvious the media were scratching for a story.

I decided to give Sergio another visit and hoped his batteries were still working and also the ones operating the radio. It was twelve noon when I arrived at the cemetery.

"Good afternoon, my little Russian friend. How are we today?"

I waited for a reply; none was forthcoming.

"Sergio, boy, are you there? You must be getting hungry by now. I have got some fish and chips here. Sorry it's not Caviar but it is the best I could do. Could you use any toilet rolls? You must be up to your eyeballs in shit by now. Last chance, are you receiving?"

There was a muffled sound.

"I can hear you. Please help me. I have Diabetes and need my medication; it is urgent."

"I have some in my car."

"Oh, the naughty boys who beat you up the day when you brought Tetyana down here to kill her. I think they have stolen it. This country is in such a state, the youths of today. I just don't know what to with them."

"Please don't, how you say, fuck me about, what do you want?"

"Where did the gold come from and where can I find Ameer?"

"The gold is easy, one of our people, he is a dirty poof. He met a man in a cottage. You know where these poofs meet. Well, he had been screwing him for weeks and another man joined them and they all got into the dirty antics together. I tell you they did it in a private room in your Parliament. Yes, he is a member of your Government. Our man then discovered that the toilet man was a criminal and knew where the gold from a robbery at Heathrow was stored. It was easy from there on. We watched the politician and found him on Hampstead Heath with another man, trousers around their ankles doing the most disgusting things to each other. He got a wonderful video and the rest was easy. We followed him to a common land, and there he was with yet another man. I explained to the politician what we wanted for the video and started to put the pressure on him. He then threatened the criminal man to tell us where certain goods were being stored. The rest was easy; the little poof after a little persuading took us to the store. I was not greedy. I only took half. It was to be my pension and then you come along and spoil it. Can we do a deal? You keep two thirds and I keep the rest and I never give you any trouble, yes?"

"Just a minute, what happened to the two homosexuals?"

"That was easy; they both died on Hampstead Heath as a result of, how do you call it a Homophobic attack. The police never found the people and to be quite honest, I do not think they try too hard. You understand? Now what about the deal?"

"Let me think about it, but first Ameer. Where can I meet him and when?"

"I can tell you he will be in Palma Mallorca for the New Year celebrations. He sails in there every year for the big celebrations. He goes on his yacht, Croesus. He has the girls delivered on the first day in January for his big party that night. He sleeps on the yacht on the last day of the year He likes to watch the big firework show. Why do you ask?"

"Oh nothing really, I just want to see him feed the seagulls."

"Seagulls, he doesn't feed birds."

"He may, but before I leave you. I would like to play you a little story."

I switched on the recording of him raping Vesta and played it over the radio to him. After a little while, the tape finished.

He tried to say something but the radio went dead. I threw the fish and chips into the bushes and dropped the wrappers into a rubbish bin.

Croesus, where had I heard that name before? I knew he was about a rich man who was noted for his great wealth and had died B.C.; this was from my school days but that name had come up recently, but where? I drove back home and searched through all the paper work connected to this job. Eventually whilst looking through the little floral diary that Farquar-Brown had given to me was the word CROESUS. Has Ameer been collecting girls every year and if so, what was he doing with them when he was finished with them?

Whatever he was doing, he had to be stopped, but how?

Chapter 37
Let's Remove the Evidence

I searched through anything that could incriminate me. I still had the passport of a Vesta and Tetyana. I could not hand them back as both girls would start to ask questions as to where I had found them, which could be rather embarrassing. Fortunately, I had always handled them whilst wearing surgical gloves. One problem I did have was the gold in the garage that would have to wait until a later day.

I purchase a padded envelope from the local post office and scribbled Vesta's address on the front and posted the two passports from a post box in Dummer.

The following day, I picked up Tom's car, filled it with petrol and collected him from Heathrow Airport. He had a broad smile on his suntanned face enhanced by the white cowboy Stetson hat he was wearing as he was pushed through the arrivals area in an airport wheelchair.

"Hi, partner."

Tom had picked up the language after two weeks.

"I see you had a good time?"

"Yes, partner and the lovely Cheryl made me most welcome."

"I take it you didn't get married in one of those Vegas marriage chapels?"

"No, Siree had the honeymoon first."

The area filled with Tom's laughter as he rocked back and forward in his chair and reverted back to his Berkshire accent.

"Got you going there, mate, come on let's get to the car. I'm knackered."

We were soon in Wokingham and Tom was tucked up in bed with the jet lag catching up. I got the impression he hadn't had too much sleep over the past few weeks.

I caught up with some housework and then settled down to watch some television. Soon I too was sound asleep. I wakened with a start. It was twelve midnight. I crept from the chair and made my way to bed.

It was seven a.m. when I opened my eyes. Soon I was up, showered and making some breakfast. After about an hour, my phone rang.

"Bob MacInally?"

"Bob, it's me, Vesta."

"Hi there, how are things?"

"Great, I have my passport."

"Where did you find it?"

"No, I did not find, it arrived in the post this morning and Tetyana's too, is that not wonderful?"

"Yes, wonderful, who sent them to you?"

"I don't know; no letter, nothing."

"Maybe Sergie?"

"Why would he send them back to me?"

"There was a story in a newspaper saying the police were looking for a Russian man who they thought had run off to Russia, perhaps he hopes you will not go to the police if you get your passport back?"

"I would not go to police and if I do, he or his friends kill my family or tell them I am a prostitute; that would kill my family, you know the disgrace."

"Does Tetyana know you have her passport?"

"No, I will have to tell her boyfriend; you know the caretaker at the flats."

"Vesta, I will come to your house this afternoon, if that is okay?"

"Yes, no problem; about four?"

"That's fine, four o'clock it is."

I travelled into London by train and was soon at Vesta's flat. I pushed the entry system button. She immediately answered; the lock clicked. The door opened and I stepped inside. It was all a too familiar sight but with a different atmosphere from my first visit, where my life was to change forever.

I stood in the vestibule and looked up the staircase to the landing where Vesta was standing. Her face was radiant as she beckoned me up the stairs. As I reached the landing, she threw her arms around me and gave me a 'bear hug'.

"Come in, I have made some coffee." She let me go and ushered me to the settee.

"Oh, Bob. I am so happy I have my passport. Soon I get a job and get money then I can go home to see my mother, father, brother and sister. I want to get away before the Russian comes back."

"I don't think he will come back if the police are looking for him. Besides what he was doing was done without the knowledge of his Embassy. Did he ever tell you what he did?"

"No, but months ago, he left papers here in an envelope. I looked at them. They were all in English with writing on them. They were about submarines in Scotland; I did not understand them but they were marked Secret. I read it says something about parliament and I think triangles. There were lots of, how do you say maps, drawings like you know, plans for houses."

"Triangles? Could it have been Trident?"

"Perhaps, I only know he was very angry that he had left the envelope by mistake. When he came back for it, he held my face very tight and asks me if I opened and read. I say no. He says you're a dead person if you have. He was very angry."

"Yes, I should think he was. I will take the phone apart to remove my equipment."

Picking up the phone, I removed the base plate and retrieved the 'bug'.

"I hope he will not come back; I look out of window to make sure, yes?"

"Yes, okay but I am sure he will not come back."

I hated lying to her, but there was no way I could tell her. This had to be my secret.

"Bob, he never brought the key back. Did you ever find out where it was for?"

"No, I never did. I suppose he must have thrown it away by now."

I finished removing the 'bug' from the telephone and replaced the base plate.

"Is the caretaker in his flat?"

"No, this is his day off. I saw him going out some time ago. I suppose he will have gone to the pub. That's what he does on his day off."

"Vesta, you can come away from the window I have finished."

"Is everything okay?"

"Yes, all done. There are so many pubs around here I suppose he has a different one each time?"

"No, I do not think so. He took me to his favourite pub one day. It was the something called Arms."

"The Cooper's Arms?"

"Yes, that's it; The Cooper's Arms, a very old pub."

I thanked her for the coffee and said my good byes.

I was soon on my way to the Cooper's Arms in Flood Street Chelsea.

Chapter 38
I Would Like an Introduction

There was a drizzle in the evening air wetting the Chelsea streets as I made my way to the pub on the corner of Redesdale Street and Flood Street. Pushing open one of the double doors, I entered a very old pub dating back to eighteen seventy-four. The air was filled with tobacco smoke from cigarettes, cigars and pipes. Numerous old oak tables were situated around the pub. They matched in with the very old wide floor boards, which looked as if they had been there since the day the pub had been built.

Standing in small groups around the tables were customers, some having what looked like serious conversations whilst others just laughing and joking. The beer was taking effect but I could not see George. After ordering and paying for a pint of their best bitter, my attention was drawn to four framed 'JAK' cartoons on the wall next to one of the large picture windows. 'JAK' was Raymond Jackson who drew cartoons for the London Evening Standard Newspaper from nineteen fifty-two and was described by Prime Minister Tony Blair as one of Britain's 'finest political cartoonists'. As I studied the characters in the drawings, I was disturbed by a male voice.

"What brings you in here?"

I looked down. It was George sitting at the table next to me. He pushed his unfinished crossword to one side of the table.

"Hi, George. I was told you might be in here."

"You've been speaking to Vesta."

"Yeah, I popped in to see her and she said you might be in here as it was your day off."

"Popped in to see her? I'll bet you did." He had a wry smile on his face.

"No, honestly, she's too young for me. Anyway, are you ready for another pint? I see that one has almost gone."

"Well, I'll have one for the road."

I made my way to the bar and ordered whatever George was having. The barmaid smiled at me and poured his favourite tipple; she poured a pint for me and I paid, collected the pints and made my way towards George.

"Here we are; she seems to know your tipple."

"Yes, I have known her for years. Strangers coming in here think she is 'crumpet'. She is a happily married woman with two kids and would never stray."

The next couple of hours were spent talking about every subject under the sun. When I thought the time was right, I brought up the subject that had brought me there.

"George, do remember we had a chat about your former officer who was running a security outfit?"

"Yeah, he was in charge of a unit down in Hereford, did his time and then got out of the outfit. He does a lot of different jobs for all sorts of people. Why do you ask?"

"I would like to have a meeting with him. I may have a bit of business I could put his way. Do you still see him?"

"As a matter of fact, I was with him in the Union Jack Club south of the water the other day. Do you want me to get him to give you a ring? It's just he does not give out his phone number."

"Yeah, I would be grateful if you could; what's his name?"

"He was Mister Roberts the last time I spoke to him."

George laughed; he knew I did not believe him.

I handed him my card. We finished our drinks and went our separate ways.

I waited for the call.

Chapter 39
One Last Visit

One week passed before I returned to the cemetery. I did not expect to have any communication with my prisoner and I was correct. I transmitted a couple of times without success. There was no reply, not even the squelch sound of an attempt to make contact. I guessed his batteries had run out, not on the radio but his body batteries. If the diabetes hadn't got him, the lack of food and water would have. Well, at least his family would not have any burial costs. I walked towards the tomb and checked the bottom of the staircase; the ground remained undisturbed. I left the area and made my way back to my car. How did I feel? To be honest, I felt very little. He was where he deserved and the world would have been a better place had he been there years before and some innocent young girls would be living with their parents or perhaps married with their own children. One down and Megan would have a lot of explaining to do to walk away from her situation.

Oh, we'll I'm getting hungry and I have got another person to get 'sorted'.

Let's hope that phone call comes in soon.

Chapter 40
Hello, Mister Roberts Here

I was in process of smashing my part of the two-way radio with a club hammer on the concrete floor of my garage when my phone rang.

"Bob, MacInally speaking."

"Hello, Mister MacInally, my name is Roberts. I was given your name by a mutual friend. I understand you may have some business that I may be able to assist you with?"

"Yes, it is of a very confidential nature and I would prefer to meet you and discuss it then. I never discuss business over the phone."

"Ah, good, a man after my own heart, I am out of the country at the moment. I will be back in a few days and I will contact you then."

"That's fine. I will speak to you then, bye."

I put the phone back in my pocket and returned to smashing the two-way radio. That completed, I started my grindstone and cut into the working end of the Mausoleum key until it was reduced to a pile of dust. I then collected a few empty wine bottles and made my way to the local 'bottle bank' taking the remains of the radio with me. The dust from the key I scattered out of my car window as I drove into town. At the bottle bank, I dropped the bottles in together with the radio parts and the rest of the key. I was aware that the collection truck would arrive, pick up the metal container and then pull a lever and the contents would spew out into the wagon for melting down at the recycling depot.

Things were much the same at home apart from the gold in the garage. I would have to store that some other place preferably abroad. Elensa had returned home to visit her family. I was at a bit of a loose end. I seemed to spend my life sitting in front of the TV watching all sorts of rubbish. Things changed one evening when the Crimewatch Programme came on the television; it opened up with the presenter making an appeal for nine missing foreign girls. The presenter gave their correct dates of birth together with their photographs. I recognised them at once. They were taken from the passports I had left in the mini bus at Heathrow Airport. Police had obviously been searching for them without success. Very few details were being given other than to say this was connected to an ongoing murder enquiry.

Had all these girls been killed by Ameer to satisfy his sadistic sexual pleasure?

My gut feeling was telling me these poor girls would never be found. The programme usually has an update some hours later. When the update came on, they once again appealed for help in tracing the girls. It was obvious they were not having any success in tracing them. As the programme finished, the usual telephone contact numbers appeared on the title. I hoped that some good would come of it but I had my doubts.

There was nothing else for me to do; so it was off to bed.

Chapter 41
At Last the Call Comes In

"Mister MacInally?"

"Speaking."

"Mister Roberts speaking, I am back in the UK, London to be precise. Perhaps we can meet up when you are free."

"I am free most days. I'll fit in with you."

"How about this evening?"

"Yes, that's fine, you say where."

"Do you know the Selfridge Hotel, just off Oxford Street in the West End of London?"

"Yes, I know it."

"There is a bar on the first floor. I think it is called Stoves. Shall we meet there at seven? Our mutual friend gave me your description; see you then." And with that, he hung up.

It was six forty-five when I walked into the hotel foyer and was directed to the far end of the first-floor lounge area and Stoves Bar. No sooner had I sat down when a small dapper man walked over to me with outstretched right hand.

"Mister MacInally?"

"Yes, Mister Roberts?"

"Yes, just call me Frank."

"Fine. I'm Bob, nice to meet you."

I ordered a round of drinks and after a short time, we got down to business. I explained the basic details of the story sticking to the Ameer side.

"Sounds like a nasty piece of shit and requires a good hiding or more."

"I was thinking more than a good hiding."

"If I am reading you correctly, you are looking for a surgical strike and termination."

"Exactly."

"These things can be done, but as you will appreciate being an ex-cop, they are not exactly legal unless a government is instructing us, and even then, they are not always legal depending on the country we are working for, and I would point out these services are not cheap."

"I have done my homework and it would appear that this guy can only be pinned down when he berths his ocean-going yacht in Palma Mallorca over the New Year period when he ties up there. On shore, he normally travels in his armoured Rolls Royce, which is carried on the ship until it is required. He also has an on-board helicopter, which I am told he does not use in Mallorca. I appreciate you do not know me from 'Adam' and you would require substantial funds on account. If you decide to undertake this, I will be paying in gold ingots."

"I will have to give this a lot of thought before I make a decision. I am sure you understand."

"Yes, fully, and as a token of my good will, I would like you to accept this gift box of Cognac." I handed him a Harrod's store bag.

"There was no need for that, Bob."

"Yes, it's only a little, but I felt I had to show you I was talking in good faith and by the way, I have removed the bottle for storage at my place. I have replaced it with a gold ingot for you to keep and have valued."

"Despite what they say about you 'Jocks', you're not tight and I have always found you to be trustworthy until you are double crossed and then the William Wallace bit comes out. Bob, I will be in touch."

With that, he picked up the carrier bag shook my hand and walked out of the bar. I finished my drink, paid the bill and left.

I was feeling good.

Chapter 42
The Job Is On!

It was seven days later when I received the call I had been waiting for.

"Good day, Bob, Frank here."

"Oh, hi Frank, how are you?"

"Yeah, I'm fine, can we have another meeting, say tomorrow or Tuesday?"

"Tomorrow is fine by me."

"That suits me. Shall we say six o'clock at the same location?"

"Yes, that is okay. Six o'clock it is then."

"Cheers, see you then."

It was with trepidation that I arrived at the meeting; basically, I hadn't a clue who he was, was I walking into a trap or was the whole thing a confidence trick?

Frank was waiting for me as I entered Stoves Bar; he stood up and shook my hand. It was a firm grip not like that 'wally' Farquar-Brown who had got me into this in the first place, or had he? If I had minded my own business, I would not have been in this situation, but then again, I had spent my working life minding other folk's business so I suppose old habits die hard; anyway, I'm here now.

"Well, Bob, I have done some research on you and I am satisfied as to who and what you are. I believe George the porter has told you a little of my background. He's a good man and a bloody good soldier. I would have had him in my Regiment if it had not been for his injury."

"He seems to be a first-class chap."

"Well, Bob, if I am taking on this job, I will have to have as much information as possible about the person in question. I will tell you at this stage I will have to be satisfied in my own mind that the operation is justified. I will not be the operative. It will be another party who will do the operation. So if you are agreeable, I will require full details of the person in question. You must write the details on a plain piece of paper. I don't have to tell you to write on a hard surface.

Do not use a pad where impressions can be traced. How soon can you do this and deliver it to me, and most of all, not a word to anyone including George."

We had a number of meetings over the next few weeks during which time I supplied Frank with as much information as I had on Ameer and the Croesus.

He confirmed the value of the gold ingot I had given him was about five hundred thousand pounds and to complete the job, he would require a further four or the equivalent in cash; two thirds before the job and the rest on a successful completion.

He had obviously carried out a lot of enquiries into both Ameer and the Croessus. He informed me he would be prepared to have his contacts under take the, as he put it the 'assignment'.

Apparently, Ameer was hated by the Israelis; they had already made one attempt on his life where two of his bodyguards had been killed. The Israelis as usual denied any involvement in this assassination attempt.

It would appear that Sergio's information was correct and a berth had been booked for her to tie up from December 28 until January 2.

Frank agreed to be paid in the gold ingots later. The team who would carry out the operation would be led by a man called Norman and his code word would be 'Palm tree'; he would make contact directly with me. No payments were to be made to him and there would be no contact to him.

The arrangements for the transportation of the gold were as follows. My instructions were to photograph and measure the size of my freezer and give the details to Frank at the next meeting. At that meeting, Frank instructed me he would order an identical freezer. This would be delivered to my house. I had to take mine to the inside of my garage and put in the appropriate number of gold ingots and secure the door closed shut with 'gaffer' tape. At a prearranged time, one of his men would arrive in a white four-ton truck and deliver the new freezer. As part of the service, the 'defective' freezer would be taken away for recycling.

It was about one week later when Frank phoned to say the new freezer would be delivered in twenty-four hours at ten o'clock in the morning. I emptied my freezer and took it into the garage where I counted the gold ingots into it and secured the door with the 'gaffer' tape and waited.

Sure enough, right on time, the van arrived outside my house (if only all deliveries were timed as perfectly) the driver in white overall and clipboard climbed down from his cab and made his way to my front door.

"Freezer for delivery and one for disposal."

"Yeah, that's for me, hold on and I'll open the garage door."

"No problems, I will offload the delivery." And with that, he made his way to the rear of his truck. I could hear the sound of the tailgate coming down as I made my way into the garage.

As I opened the door, he was already outside with a hand 'pump up truck' inside the rear of his truck and was manoeuvring it laden with the new freezer complete with the packaging and the polythene wrapper around it onto the tailgate. At ground level, he negotiated it up my driveway, offloaded the freezer and picked up the 'old one' and put it onto the lorry, pulled down the shutter and put up the tailgate.

Handing me a receipt, which I signed, he then assisted me with the freezer into the house and we connected it to the electric supply.

Returning to his cab, he got in and drove off.

Did he realise he was carrying three quarters of a million pounds worth of gold or had I fallen for a very elaborate confidence trick?

Chapter 43
Trafficking

Three days had passed and I had not heard from Frank. To say the least I was becoming anxious. Had I put too much trust in someone I did not know?

It was mid-morning when the phone rang. I almost fell over a chair in my rush to answer it.

"Bob, MacInally."

"Hi, Bob."

It was Liz.

"Oh, hi Liz."

"Don't sound so disappointed. Waiting for a call from one of your lady friends, were we?"

"No, honestly I was waiting for a call from someone, but as usual, Liz, it's nice to hear from you. How are you doing?"

"I'm fine, I have moved to London, and I'm working for The Salvation Army full time. I am helping to run a 'safe house' for girls who have been brought into the country supposed to be for all sorts of reasons but they are being forced into the sex industry. If I were to tell you what their pimps are doing to them, you would not believe it; then again, maybe YOU would. I am living in one of the safe houses in the East End of London. Perhaps we can meet up in Central London one of these days, yes?"

"Yes, you tell me when and I will come into the West End."

"I am not working tomorrow, how does that suit you?"

"Yes, that's fine by me. You tell me where?"

"How about that café in the 'Army' place in Regent Street, you know where we met the last time?"

"Yes, that's fine by me. Shall we say three o'clock?"

"Yes, good. I will see you then, bye Bob."

"Bye."

I had been so busy dealing with Frank and the ongoing situation that I had not spoken to Elensa or Vesta for some time. I decided to walk to the coffee shop. Ordering a coffee, I picked up a newspaper from the rack and opened it with some difficulty. It had obviously been read by the various customers throughout the day. In an inside page was the heading 'Police identify missing girl'. The story went on to explain about the severed head, which had been found in Basingstoke and the subsequent arrest of a Welsh woman after the police had raided a mansion in Dummer, near Basingstoke. Detective Inspector Margaret Cassidy of the Metropolitan police said, "This enquiry will stretch worldwide and involves human trafficking. We have already found many young women, many from Eastern bloc countries who have been brought into this country on various pretexts and forced into prostitution by their gang masters." When asked how many young women had been arrested, she said, "I would prefer to use the word 'rescued' rather than arrested."

Detective Inspector Margaret Cassidy?

That was the Detective Sergeant at Chelsea Police when I was arrested, or was it? She must be on attachment from the Met. Oh, well good luck Thames Valley Police.

"You looking for Elensa?"

It was one of the waitresses.

"Yes, is she about?"

"No, she had to go back home. Her mother has been taken into hospital. She left this note for you."

I opened the envelope and read the note. It would appear that her mother had been in a car crash and had been rushed into hospital in a serious condition. Elensa had no idea when she would return to England, but said she would telephone me as soon as she had news. I felt bad that I had not been with her to at least take her to the airport. I finished my coffee and made my way home.

My telephone was ringing as I entered the hallway.

"Bob MacInally."

"Hi Bob, Frank here. I got the freezer for recycling. I trust the new one is working fine. The money was fine on the old one. Scrap metal is fetching a good price these days. Can we meet up soon to talk about business?"

"I am in London tomorrow if that is any use?"

"That's fine by me. Shall we say seven o'clock in the usual place."

"I have to meet someone at three o'clock so that suits me fine. See you then."
What a relief, he is genuine. I hope!

Chapter 44
The Rink

"Good afternoon and welcome to the Rink."

"I'm sorry, sir. I was looking for The Salvation Army."

"That's us. The Regent Hall Salvation Army."

"I thought you said 'The Rink'?"

"Yes, the building has been known as 'The Rink' since William Booth our founder bought it in 1882 when it was a skating rink and he changed it into a place of worship; it is the only church in Oxford Street."

"Oh, I see, I was looking for your café."

"No problem; let me take you to it."

He led me down a corridor and into the café where I saw Liz sitting at a table.

"Bob."

Standing up, she walked towards me, arms outstretched and gave me a 'bear hug'.

"Oh, Bob, it's great to see you. It seems ages since Puerto Pollenca, how have you been?"

"I'm fine, and you?"

"Me too, my life has been completely changed since I moved down here, anyway never mind that, let me get you a coffee."

We sat down at a table and Liz started to tell me about her life working in the safe house for as she put it 'working girls'.

"Life dealt me a funny hand of cards. I am glad to be away from my past life up north but now I find myself trying to help girls from my past life. When I was doing the business, to a certain extent it was my choice. Admittedly, I was forced into it by the guy I was with at the time but most of the girls I come into contact with at the house are a long way from home in a strange land. Some of them were being raped sometimes up to ten times a day. They were kept locked up in flats and not allowed out. Most of them are from around the Russia area and are sold to guys over here who run them. They seem to start off as so called 'escorts' for rich guys who think nothing of paying at least a thousand pounds a time. That kind of life, what with the drugs they put into them and the abuse the take from the punters, soon tells on them and once the makeup is washed off the wear and tear soon shows. That is when they are put into 'Sauna Massage' so called parlours. Some of these kids have at least fifteen clients a day. One of the girls once told me she heard two of her 'pimps' talking saying it was easier money than drugs as a junky will pay twenty-five pounds for a fix and a punter at the Sauna may pay fifty to a hundred a time and guys are queuing up to be next into the room."

Memories of my man from the grave came flooding back.

"You looked shocked, Bob."

"No, not really. It is just that I was never involved in this type of work when I was in the job. Although back in the seventies, some bent senior officers were making a fortune on 'back handers' from these types of guys who were mostly Maltese. Mind you, it was straight cops who nicked the bent cops and got them banged up for years."

"Yeah, in this life, for every bad person, there are hundreds of good ones. Wouldn't you agree?"

"Yes, I would but, the people I came into in the biggest part of my police service were down right bad. Now you take the ones that put the girls you're dealing with into that situation I can only consider them to be bad."

"Some people would consider my past life as bad."

"You were doing a bad job but I would never consider you to be a bad person because of what you were doing; your ponce he was bad and likewise the guy who gave you a hiding and left you for dead in an alleyway."

"Then Major Mary, a good person came along and changed me by introducing me to God and the Bible. You didn't expect to hear that from me did you Bob? Now be honest."

"No, not really, but I must say I have seen a remarkable change in you for the better."

"Well, Bob, I don't go about shouting my mouth off about the change in my life I just hope people can see something in me that makes them realise there is a better way. Nobody at the house knows about me doing the business in 'The Pool'. Although some of the girls are amazed at my knowledge of 'the game'. I pray for them every day and trust that they can be reunited with their families.

Most are only kids. The youngest girl we are looking after is only fifteen years. The police found her working in a brothel in the West End, she is so traumatised she doesn't know anything about her past."

I thought I had seen a lot in my life but the more I thought of these things the more I wanted to meet Frank and get matters sorted. I had a few more coffees with Liz and I made my way out of the Salvation Army and down Oxford Street. Killing some time, I walked into Selfridges the large store in the north side of the street. The time passed. I left the store and walked to the hotel and made my way through the lounge and into Stoves bar. Frank was sitting in the corner with a 'gin and tonic' on his table. Thumbing through the Daily Telegraph newspaper, he stood up, hand outstretched, we shook hands.

"Hi, Bob, how are things?"

"Yes, fine. I trust the freezer was okay?"

"Absolutely fine. All in working order and will be put to good use. Here let me get you a drink." And with that, he ordered a drink from the waiter.

It soon arrived and we got down to business.

"When the time comes, my man will meet you in Mallorca at Palma Cathedral at a time to be arranged. He will fill you in on the procedures and supply you with the necessary equipment. He will have taken care of everything else. On December 31, you will be a few hundred yards away from the location getting ready for the large firework display to bring in the New Year. I would suggest you should be in Mallorca from say, December 25 until say January 8. That will let you take in the New Year celebrations and the traditional Three Kings mass and celebrations. Book Charter flights and a good hotel in Palma, pay by card not cash, that always raises suspicions, as I am sure you are aware."

"So as I understand it your man will prepare everything."

"Correct."

"I would have preferred to have been out of town for the event."

"Don't worry nothing will come back to you, I promise. Just one last question, do you have a foreskin?"

"Your guy's not gay, is he?"

"Far from it, all will become clear when you meet him."

"I am intrigued."

"I will contact you in one week and then we can meet and I will give you the final details. In the meantime, book flights and accommodation."

We went our separate ways and I started to have second thoughts. Was I doing the right thing? If didn't do it then who would? I consoled myself by thinking what that louse had done to the poor girls and would continue to do so if not stopped.

Weeks passed and I still had not heard from Elensa nor had any one at the coffee shop, I could only guess she must be still at home with her mother.

Reports appeared in the press and on television that Megan Jones had been charged with the murder of Nadya and the three Russian men who had been arrested with her at the airport had also been charged with various offences including conspiracy to kidnap. I assumed that this referred to the girls they had brought into the country. Hints were made that police were still searching for another Russian man who had frequently been seen driving his Mercedes car to and from the mansion in Dummer.

I thought to myself 'you will have a long search'.

My main concern was how was I going to get the gold in my garage to a safe storage area where I could eventually change it into cash.

Time passed and I eventually booked my flight and accommodation for my 'festive season' in Mallorca.

Another meeting took place with Frank who gave me some details.

"Right, Bob, here we are. I want you to take this mobile with you it is on the Spanish network and not registered to anyone. Switch the phone on, and on December 28 after ten a.m., you will receive a text message wishing you a happy birthday on your fourteenth. That will refer to fourteen hundred hours on the twenty second when my man will meet you. You must go to Palma Cathedral. Enter by the front door and walk down the aisle towards the High Altar where you should sit on the last pew on the right. My man will approach you and talk about the architecture; this will give you the opportunity to introduce the code word which I am sure you have remembered?"

"I remember palm tree, and he is Norman, correct?"

"Correct."

"How will he recognise me? Should I wear something special?"

"No, don't worry about that he has already seen you."

I did not ask any questions; it was obvious his team had done their homework.

"Both of you will then leave the Cathedral and have a walk. He will fill you in on the final details and supply you with a piece of equipment. Once you have completed the briefing, you will be left with the phone. You will not be able to contact him; any contact made will be from him."

I gave him the dates when I would be in Mallorca and we said our farewells and made our separate ways.

The only thing left to do was count the days until it was time to leave.

Chapter 45
Festive Season

The plane touched down and taxied to its stand whilst the cabin crew welcomed us to Palma Airport 'where the outside temperature is twenty-two degrees'. The doors of the aircraft opened and the warm scented air rushed in. Soon I was in the baggage hall collecting my cases from the carousel and making my way to the queue waiting for a taxi. It was not long before I was seated in the rear of a taxi and making my way along the Avinguda Gabriel Roca to my hotel. Hanging along the streets were the illuminated 'Felices Navidad' decorations, it did not feel like Christmas to me.

I was here to kill a man.

The taxi arrived outside my hotel. I got out and carried my bags into the reception area where a porter rushed over and took them from me. After I had checked in at reception, he led me to my room. I could not help but think how similar he appeared to be like Manuel from Faulty Towers the television series as he scuttled down the corridor with my bags.

"Room tree to uno, sir, very nice room you can see big sheeps in Marina."

Putting my larger case onto the case stand. He handed me the keycard for the room.

"Have nice stay. You want anything you call me. I am Pepe I can find anything for you in Palma."

Handing him a twenty Euro note, he thanked me and reminded me he could get me anything in Palma as he shaped his hands into the shape of a female and winked at me.

"Anything."

He left, closing the door behind him. I started to unpack my case, putting clothes into the wardrobe. It was at this point I felt so lonely in a strange town with no one to talk to, thoughts rushed through my head, the guy in the tomb clawing at the metal door, trying to call out, his throat so dry he could hardly make a sound. Did he stumble and fall down the stairs to come to rest and die next to the Braithwaite family who had been gently laid to rest so many years before? There would be no rest for him; nothing but torture as he lay there thinking of his family if in fact he had any, back home in Russia. I sat on the bed my head in my hands as I played these thoughts over and over in my mind. With a start, I jumped up and came to my senses. I immediately thought of poor Nadya being hacked to pieces and her young head thrown onto a council tip to be mixed into a load of families household waste, no that bastard got all he deserved.

Smiling to myself, I thought of Megan and how she must have felt when she was shown the exhibit bags containing Nadya's clothing and the Ozi, in my mind I could imagine her response.

"It's a fit up; you bastards have fitted me up."

Then I thought of the Investigating Officer talking to her.

"How do you account for your DNA being on her clothes and on the knife and saw that you used to cut the poor girls body to pieces?"

She must have been pulling her hair out as she sat in her lonely cell. I'll bet she puts the 'fit up' down to Sergio, her late lover, who had vanished off the scene.

I felt so much better after I had thought it over. It was like when I was a kid on holiday in Scotland dressed in loose fitting swimming trunks and stepping into the ice-cold river Clyde at Dunoon with my mother telling me to get into the water as I would be okay when the water came up to my shoulders. This was the same feeling. Once I looked at the full story, I felt much better and I was in this up to my neck.

But what about Ameer?

Chapter 46
Sacred Music

The next few days were spent walking around Palma and changing my US Dollars into Euros at various Bureau de Change outlets and I became a 'tourist' visiting many tourist spots including a trip to Soller on the mountain train.

Time passed and on the morning of December 28, I switched on the phone Frank had given me, at eleven a.m. a text message came in; 'Wishing you all the best on your fourteenth birthday…Granpa xx'.

I walked into the town centre and 'killed' some time in cafes and Corte de Ingles in the Avinguda de James 111 looking at goods I had no intention of buying. Eventually as the time for my 'meet' approached, I made my way out of the store and walked down towards the Cathedral and through the front door and down the aisle, eventually sitting in the front pew. With my head bowed and my eyes closed as the sacred music played quietly throughout the Cathedral, I found myself praying silently to myself. As I slowly opened my eyes, I became aware of a man sitting close by. He was aged about fifty years of age. I guessed he was about five feet eight inches tall or slightly smaller. There was not an ounce of fat on him and in fact, he looked remarkably fit for his age, our eyes made contact.

"Wonderful architecture, they knew how to build things in those days."

"Yes, they certainly did."

Was this Norman or could it be a chance that the man had used the code unwittingly?

"Mind you the Spanish always take the easy way out and yet their work always turns out first class. I have just watched a lorry unload six fully grown Palm trees outside the Cathedral."

"You must be Bob."

He reached out his right hand and we shook hands.

"Norman?"

"That's me, pleased to meet you."

He moved closer to me.

"Let's sit for a couple of minutes and then we will take a walk."

We sat talking and pointing out parts of the ceiling which neither of us knew the first thing about. Standing up, we turned left through the Cloisters and out of the Cathedral as we did so one of the fathers gave us a sickly smile. Before I could say anything, Norman whispered.

"He thinks his luck is in. He thinks we are a couple of old shirt lifters."

Once into the street, Norman started to fill me in on the operation.

"We have checked out the arrival of Croesus. Her arrival will be on the twenty-eighth at about twelve noon. The berth where she ties up is one of the few where you can drive your car up to the gangplank or whatever they call it these days. Immediately next to this is a concrete cabinet with a glass front; inside is a fire extinguisher on a trolley. It is about three feet tall. It will be doctored by us and will have a radio receiver attached to it. To trigger the device, you will use this."

He then produced a leather cigar holder and slid the outer case off. Inside the tops of five cigars were exposed.

Pointing to a cigar on the right of the case, he offered it to me.

"Here, take this one."

I took the cigar that he had indicated and held it in my hand, he removed another that had been next to it and put it in his mouth and lit it. He held the light towards me. Slipping the cigar into my mouth, he lit it.

"They are the best Havanas, all down to expenses. Now look at the three cigars that are left; the two nearest to the empty spaces are genuine and ready cut. Now this one (pointing to the one on the left of the holder) is not."

Taking hold of it, he slowly unscrewed it; it was metal made to look like a cigar. After removing the 'metal cigar', he held the leather case open to show me what looked like an old-fashioned typewriter key at the top.

"When this is depressed, this will operate the radio signal which will trigger the fire extinguisher. It will operate over a distance of five hundred yards max. It works perfectly at four hundred we have tested it."

We continued walking towards the harbour to a spot about a mile from the Cathedral and along the front where there were many cafes and tourist 'pirate ships'.

"Now when you reach this point outside this hotel, look out to sea through the walkways to the ships you can see two cranes, yes?"

"Yes, I can see them."

"Now come with me across the road and sit on the concrete bench. From here, you will get a perfect view as his car arrives next to the Croesus. When he steps out of the car, that is when you press the button in the cigar case. There will be a large bang. There will be lots of people standing around waiting for the fireworks to commence. Screw the cover over the button and walk off into the crowd; the fireworks will last for about forty minutes; the ships horns will sound for about one minute to welcome in the New Year. I would suggest you arrive in the area fifteen minutes before midnight, assuming you are correct with the times you will see his car come off the road and drive along the Jetty. After you have used the cigar holder, remove a cigar, light it up to welcome in the New Year. Do not be tempted to walk on the footway on the harbour side as this covered by CCTV, now here's two cigars to replace the two we used."

We walked back towards the Cathedral. We agreed we would not meet again; I would keep the phone switched off until December 31, the cigar holder's battery had a life of three weeks. Both were to be destroyed as quickly as possible on January 1.

I returned to my hotel and put the equipment into my room safe. I hired a car and the next few days were spent touring around the Island. I returned to my hotel on the thirtieth at about seven p.m., had a meal and then walked along the harbour front towards the hotel and the two cranes. On reaching there, I looked to my left and there she was, Croesus fully flood lit and tied up in the berth Norman had pointed out, she was a magnificent ship, dark-blue in colour with three decks and a helicopter on the helicopter pad on the stern. Her sleek lines made her stand out amongst other ships moored nearby.

I was tempted to have a closer look but remembered Norman's advice, 'there is CCTV on that side'. I was soon back into my bed and fast asleep.

I was amazed when I wakened to discover it was seven a.m. I removed the phone from the safe and switched it on. There were no messages. After breakfast, I sat in the lounge reading a book until mid-afternoon. The time could not pass quick enough for me. I returned to my room and collected the cigar holder and made my way along the seafront and had a meal in a local restaurant. I sipped a couple of glasses of wine; most of the clients were dressed in their 'Sunday best' and were obviously prepared to make a night of it.

Eleven thirty eventually arrived and I made my way towards Croesus.

Arriving outside the hotel, I lined up my line of sight between the two cranes. There she was, perfectly in the position. At eleven forty-five, I crossed the road towards the concrete bench, as I did so a chauffeur driven Rolls Royce drove past me and turned left in towards the security gates entrance. A security guard walked towards the car the windows were lowered and the guard looked in, stepped back and saluted. Sitting in the rear of the car was a big fat Arab smoking a large cigar.

Cigar! I fumbled and with shaking hands, I removed the cigar case from my pocket and slid the outer case off. Unscrewing the 'cigar' on the left as I watched the 'Roller' slowly make its way towards the gangplank. The driver got out and walked around to open the passenger's door; as soon as he did, the Arab stepped out and looked about with an air of arrogance as if examining his kingdom. I put my finger on the button and pressed.

Nothing!

He turned and started to walk towards the ship.

I pressed harder. There was a blinding flash which lit up the sky and was eerily reflected in the clouds, then there was a pause followed by a deafening thud as the sky again lit up in a bright yellow cloud followed by black smoke.

The crowds on the hotel balconies cheered thinking they were bringing in the New Year. I stood up and crossed the road back towards the hotel. Guests were checking their watches and comparing the time with each other. It was then all hell broke loose as the sky over the bay was filled with exploding fireworks and the ships horns were blasting in the New Year. All around, people were hugging and kissing each other and anyone who were within their reach. Screwing the top over the button on the cigar case I pulled out a cigar lit it up and walked off in the direction of the Cathedral. I listened for the sound of emergency sirens without success. I was greeted by so many people, many Brits as I walked by the cafes as the clients spilled out onto the footway. By the time I reached my hotel, I had lost count of how many glasses of wine I had drunk.

When I arrived back at my hotel, a party was in full swing. I returned to my room and deposited the phone and cigar case in the safe. Returning downstairs, I joined the party until three a.m. when I went to my room and 'crashed out' on top of my bed.

Chapter 47
It's on the News

I wakened at nine a.m. fully clothed. It was then the events of the previous night hit me as I drank glass after glass of water partially to quench my thirst and to get rid of the taste of the cigar. I checked the safe to make sure the equipment was still inside. After showering and getting dressed, I walked to a local café and tried to eat some breakfast washed down with coffees. The television news was on showing the celebrations from the night before. There was no news of the Croesus.

I walked back to the hotel and collected the telephone and cigar case, as I stepped into the lift I met two middle aged women.

"Hi there, if it isn't John Travolta."

It all came flooding back. They were my dance partners from the night before.

"Thanks for the Champagne, Bob, you know how to treat a lady. One bottle would have been more than enough, but thanks anyway. We will repay you tonight, eight o'clock in the bar. See you then."

They got out on the second floor.

Their words flowed through my fuzzy mind. "John Travolta? How many bottles?"

Time to get out and get some fresh air. Getting into the car, I put the phone and cigar case into the glove compartment and drove off towards the Cap de Formentor at the north of the Island. After about an hour, I was passing Puerto Pollensa where this had all started. All as the result of buying a second-hand book. I started to climb up the mountain above the bay and the military base where, for years, tourists had looked in awe as the Seaplane flew down and scooped up gallons of water to fly to some forest fire or on occasions when training the water load would be dropped back into the Mediterranean Sea, much to the enjoyment of all the children.

This was no time to daydream. I had serious things to do. The road continued turning and twisting high above the luxurious Formentor hotel and the many luxurious villas owned by some of the richest people in the world.

After about another forty minutes, I reached a parking place about a quarter of a mile from the lighthouse at the end of the road.

Despite the time of year, it was still very warm. Reaching into the glove compartment, I removed the cigar case and the telephone and stepped out into the heat of the day. I walked away from the car towards the direction of the cliff edge. Sitting down at a suitable point, I removed the phone and cigar case and then smashed both to pieces between two rocks and started throwing the pieces over the cliff edge into the foaming sea many metres below. I made sure there was nothing left on the ground and made my way back to the car watched by one of the mountain goats standing nearby. Thank the Lord he can't speak.

It was about another twenty minutes when I found myself back in Puerto Pollensa, which appeared deserted as most of the shops were closed. Eventually, I found the Pub Imperial in the Paseo Saralegui open. It is a small bar situated on the sea front. There were a few tourists sitting outside having a drink.

"Hi there, back again."

I looked around. It was a couple I knew by sight but never had anything to do with. To be quite honest, they were a couple of old 'soaks' on the island for the cheap booze.

"Come on sit, doon, there's naebody sittin' there."

Why does this type of person have to talk like Glasgow 'cave dwellers' despite the fact they are hundreds of miles from their caves?

"Stayin' the port?"

"No, not this time, just passing through."

"Aye, right where are you stayin?"

Trying to avoid conversation, I looked at both of them.

"Palma, just came over for the Christmas and New Year celebration."

She looked at me through her bloodshot eyes.

"Big firework thingy thing there last night. Did yi see it?"

"Could not miss it."

Before I could say anything more, he butted in.

"Aye, a guy got killed there last night, it was on the tele, said a big box of squibs blew up and that was him deid. Fancy that at 'Nerday' tae. Heah, brought the New Year in wae a bang. Get it?"

Fire point in Palma, where bomb was planted

I got it okay; the owner arrived with my glass of Coke.

"Heh, Pepe, I was just tellin' this guy, whit's your name?"

"Bob."

"A' was sayin' tae Bob a guy got blown up in Palma last night."

The owner stopped at the table next to where I was sitting, putting his tea towel over his shoulder he joined in the conversation.

"It has just been on the television news. The top police boss from Palma says it was a bomb, here come through it's on television now."

We walked through the small bar to the end where a television was showing pictures of a burnt-out car and an area surrounded by plastic police tape; the camera then panned around to show the stern of the ship with her name 'CROESUS'. The reporter pointed to the concrete base of what appeared to have been where a fire extinguisher had been stored. There were a lot of passers by being interviewed and then the film cut to other events.

The barman started to translate for us.

"The police say the ship was owned by a very rich Arab and they think a bomb had been left in a large fire extinguisher and someone made it go bang and killed the man whose body had been blown to pieces. Police divers were searching for body parts but were having problems with sea birds removing the parts. They don't know who did it but were checking every one leaving Palma Airport."

With that, the Glasgow couple came out with their theories. He started.

"I will bet you it's the Jews. They don't like Arabs. You know what I mean. The ones who did it will be pissin' it up in Jerusalem by now, all tell you they are well gone by now, that's how they dae things."

That was his comments on world affairs. He was rudely interrupted by his wife.

"Get oot yi wee bastard."

Her husband sprang into action.

"Whit's up, Agnes?"

"There's a bastard fly in ma San Miguel." And with that, she started to stab it with her middle finger.

I paid for my drink and returned to my car. An hour later, I was back in my hotel in Palma.

The next few days were uneventful until January 5 when the Festival of the Three Kings takes place with the highly decorated floats parading through the streets with children on board throwing sweets into the crowds lining the streets. It was a joyous celebration. My thoughts turned to the families of all the missing children who had vanished by the hands of Sergio, Megan and Ameer. At least they will not be doing any more evil in the world.

The following day, I was preparing to return on the seven p.m. flight. My cases were taken to the reception area where I commenced to check out. The receptionist reached under the reception desk.

"Mister MacInally, your passport, the police were in copying all the passports, you know because of the big bomb. The policeman, Tollo, is my brother in law; he tells me you were a policeman and not Jewish. He told me not to tell anyone 'cause they have found parts of the bomb were from Israel, you know, Jewish. I tell you only because you were a policeman, but sssh."

With that, she put her index finger over her lips. I thought to myself the 'Spanish Old Bill' have done their homework on me.

Soon I was in the departure lounge in Palma Airport and then onto my flight and home to sort out the bundles of mail and Christmas cards behind the door. After couple of days, I received a call from Frank and we arranged to meet in Maggie Jones's Restaurant in Kensington a favourite for locals for the past thirty odd years. It was said it was here Princess Margaret used to meet Tony Armstrong Jones prior to their marriage. The story seemed to make sense as it was just around the corner from Kensington Palace.

Chapter 48
All Over?

We had our meeting in this cosy restaurant tucked away in a cul-de-sac between Kensington High Street and Kensington Church Street in Central London. Frank was waiting in a corner table surrounded by artifacts on the walls and ceilings.

"Hi, Bob, good holiday?"

"Yes, very good, nice change to get some decent weather at this time of year. And you?"

"Yeah met up with some old friends, they had been away for a few days mountaineering. They apparently had a good time and arrived home safely with no mishaps."

"The thing about my foreskin all falls into place now. The Jewish connection, yes."

Frank just smiled and picked up his glass of wine and reached towards me, the two glasses touched.

"Cheers."

"Cheers, I have sorted out the final part of the contract. It's in the briefcase which is under the table, don't lose it on the way home. There is something I want to ask you I hope you do not mind."

Frank looked over the top of his glass.

"Yeah go on fire away."

"Did you have any problems cashing the metal work in?"

Putting his glass slowly down on to the table, he stared straight at me.

"Why do you ask?"

"I don't want to know where or anything like that, and I'm sure you would not tell me even if I was to ask you. It is quite simple I have some I would like to cash in and if we could do some business together I would be more than happy to do the business with you."

He sat staring at the table for a few moments.

"The people I do business with are trustworthy. All I will say is my team saved the family from a terrorist group. We negotiated the ransom for their successful release and then we eliminated that particular cell. What amounts are we talking about?"

"About sixty bars."

"Bloody hell, have you done the Bank of England?"

"No, let's just say I have relieved some rather nasty people of their storage problems."

"Bob, if this stuff is of the same quality as the last lot, we are talking serious money."

I topped up our glasses and we had a mouthful each.

"It goes without saying Frank that you would be working on a percentage and likewise your people."

"I am sure I can do business with you, Bob, leave it with me and I will get back to you, okay?"

"Fine by me, cheers."

We finished off another bottle of Gevrey Chanbertin Faiveley 2008 and said our farewells. Frank walked off with the briefcase.

Inside were two gold bars. A bonus for a job well done.

Chapter 49
Guilty!

The following day, I called into the local newsagent to collect the daily papers. All the 'Redtops' were blazoned with the type of headlines we have grown to expect after an event they consider sensational if only to increase sales. My attention was drawn to one of the banner headlines 'EVIL MEGAN GUILTY'. I removed the paper and started to read the first paragraph. The Jury at Winchester Crown Court yesterday returned a verdict of 'Guilty' on evil Megan Jones from Dummer in Hampshire.

"This is not a library, you tight Scottish git."

I looked around; it was Pete the locksmith.

"How you doing, haven't seen you about, been away?"

"Yeah, I brought Christmas and the New Year in down in Spain, the weather was pretty good. How are you anyway?"

"I'm fine had a pretty quiet time the shop was open between Christmas and the New Year, the cleaning side was busy, gravy stained shirts, trousers and of course red wine over party frocks. When I look around and see the number of pissed girls in town, I am amazed. I think they must pour most of it over themselves. Anyway, it's good for business. By the way, I always meant to ask you, did that key I cut fit okay?"

I was a little taken aback.

"Yes, I sent it up to the in-laws up in Perthshire. They had bought an old property and one of the old doors in the house was locked open."

Peter looked at me a bit puzzled.

"Why didn't they just use the key they made the impression from?"

This was going to require some quick thinking.

"Oh, I thought I had told you the handle bit was missing."

Pete was in his glory now.

"Ah, you mean the shank, very unusual for that to go, never heard of that before mm."

"Well, you saved the day, Pete."

Changing the story quickly, I held the newspaper headlines up.

"I was reading about that poor kid who had been killed and the cow that did it was found guilty in court yesterday."

He took the paper from me.

"We should be hanging these bastards."

"Well, Pete as Billy Connelly says, 'hanging is too good for them it's a good kicking they need'."

Pete laughed as he handed the paper back to me.

"Trust you to have a laugh, I suppose it must have come with your old job. How you could deal with these people I'll never understand."

I took another two papers to the counter, paid for them and walked to the coffee shop for my fix of caffeine.

Sitting down with my papers and coffee, I started to read the reports on the previous days hearing at Winchester Crown Court. The case had been presided over by Judge Richard Ferguson who when sentencing Jones to life imprisonment said, "You are an evil woman and despite all the damming evidence against you, DNA and fingerprints found on the very tools you used to butcher this young girl visiting this country your defence was a pack of lies saying it was all planted in your vehicle by some Russian man whom you call Sergio Barakov." As yet, he has still to be found if he ever existed. You as I said before are a wicked evil woman.

I closed the paper and sipped my coffee.

"Good morning, Bob."

It was Elensa. I stood up almost knocking the table over.

"Elensa, I thought you were still in Latvia. I got your letter. How is your mother?"

"She is not good. I will have to go back home to look after her. I return home this Friday."

I held her arms and stared into her face.

"For how long?"

"I have no idea. My father is older than my mother and he can't look after her, now I do it for her."

She looked so worried. I didn't want her to leave but I understood.

On Friday morning, I collected her and took her to the airport. It was a very sad parting.

Then again, she may come back or was this just wishful thinking on my part?

I was becoming more anxious each day as I thought of the gold in my garage. I made enquires at a local Storage Centre and decided to rent a small unit, about the size of two phone boxes. I signed the appropriate paper work, paid for six months rental and collected my keys.

I found some empty cartons behind local shops that had contained washing machines and tumble driers they each had wooden floors and Polystyrene linings. I rented a small van and took the cartons home. Inside the cartons, I screwed plastic storage boxes to the wooden floors placing gold bars in the boxes one at a time. I tested the weight, with six inside I could just manage to lift the carton into the back of the van. The plastic box could hold a number of other bars which I then covered with 'cat litter' to stop any movement and then snapped the lid on.

It was a short trip to the Storage Centre where the assistant helped me to unload the 'washing machine' and trolley it into my unit. The tumble drier was delivered in a similar manner. The rest of the gold was delivered in numerous plastic storage boxes covered with office files. In all, it took dozens of visits to empty the garage.

I felt a sense of relief knowing that my garage was now empty of the gold.

Two weeks later, I received a call from Frank who informed me that his people were prepared to take half of all the gold I had but wanted twenty per cent of the value of the goods, the cash would be paid in Bearer Bonds or direct to any bank of my choice. I agreed to the conditions and within two days I met Frank outside the Storage Centre and the 'washing machine' was trolleyed onto the back of his vehicle.

I knew I was taking a tremendous risk handing over millions of pounds worth of gold to a comparative stranger the only thing I could do was to wait and see.

The next few weeks were spent waiting for my phone to ring. Eventually, it did ring.

"Bob MacInally."

"Hi, Bob, it's Frank. I am sorry about the delay. Everything went okay? I have got some figures for you. Can we meet and I can fill you in on the details? How about next Thursday? I am visiting Hereford on the Wednesday. Perhaps we could meet somewhere around about Reading?"

"That would be fine by me. How about The Saint Anne's Manor Hotel? it's just off the Three Two Nine as you come into Wokingham on the left-hand side, it is well sign posted. You give me a time and I'll see you there."

"That's fine by me, Bob. Shall we say three o'clock?"

"Spot on, I will see you then."

"Bye."

I felt such a sense of relief that my money was safe, my money? It certainly was not going back to the slag who had nicked it and I was sure had no use for it now. Not only that the missing gold would keep the villains busy looking for Sergio and what they believed was theirs. The one thing that puzzled me was how did that gold get into the Mausoleum?

Chapter 50
Have You Read the Newspapers?

"Bob MacInally speaking."

"Hello, Bob, it is Vesta. How are you?"

"Oh, I am fine and how are you?"

"I am okay. Have you seen the newspapers about Ameer?"

I took in a deep breath.

"No, what was that about?"

"He died."

"Died, where, how?"

"In Spain, the television say, big explosion on a ship and he killed."

"What happened, was it the engines that blew up?"

"No, no, the television say it is a big bomb that blew up as he got out of car."

"A bomb, I guess that must be the Israelis. There has always been trouble between these two countries. You know Arabs and Jews right back to the times of the Bible."

"In some ways, Bob, I am glad he has died. He was bad man. What he did to the girls was so bad. Bob, I have never seen Sergio for a long time. What do you think has happened to him?"

"I read in the newspaper that a woman he knew had gone to prison for killing Nadya and she said she had never seen him for a long time. The jury and Judge did not believe her. I think he has gone back to Russia. Did he ever bring back the key he took?"

"No, I never see it again. Did you ever make one?"

"No, there did not seem any point. Anyway, forget these bad people. What are you going to do with yourself?"

There was a long silence. I waited for a reply.

"Vesta, are you still there?"

"Yes, I am here, sorry."

It was obvious she was crying and amid the tears, she answered.

"Sorry, Bob, I just do not feel good. These people changed my life I am dirty. My life has been ruined. How can I go home and face my family. I am not the person I was when I arrived in your country. My family would not recognise me. How can I face them."

It was obvious that she was going through a terrible time emotionally.

"Vesta, will you be at the house tonight?"

"Yes, why?"

"I will come and visit you and we can go out for a meal. Would you like that?"

"Yes, that would be good."

"Okay, I will come to you about six o'clock."

"That would be nice, I will see you then."

She was very upset and the more I thought about her and how far she was far from home, I knew I had to do something but what?

As I drove into London, the answer suddenly hit me. Liz and the Salvation Army crowd she was with.

As soon as I was in London, I telephoned Liz and explained the situation to her. She said she would make enquiries and call me back.

I rang the doorbell at Vesta's flat.

"Hello."

"Hi, Vesta, it's Bob."

"Come up."

The door latch clicked open and I pushed the door closing it gently behind me as I entered the hall. Vesta was standing on the first-floor landing. I waved to her and walked up the stairs. She smiled through her grief torn face.

"Bob, come in and I will make a coffee."

I followed her into the kitchen. Her hands shook as she poured the water into the mugs.

I took the coffee from her shaking hands and we walked through into the living room.

"I am sorry I have no biscuits; I have not been out to shops."

"Now tell me, Vesta, what is wrong?"

She burst into tears, sobbing and at the same time trying to get her breath. I am no expert but it was clear that she needed some form of medical help and counselling.

"Have you eaten?"

"No, I am not hungry."

"Well, Vesta, I am. Why don't you go and get your coat on and we will have a walk down the road and have a snack in a café, the fresh air, if there is any in London, will do us good, okay?"

"Okay, let me get ready."

She stood up and started to pick up the coffee mugs. One slipped from her hands spilling the coffee remains onto the table top. This brought on another flood of tears.

"Leave that, you go and get ready and I will clean it up."

"Sorry, sorry, I did not mean it."

I took her arm and helped her up from the settee; her body was shaking as I did so. Letting her go she walked towards the toilet. Picking up the mugs, I walked into the kitchen. It was clean and tidy. I opened the dishwasher door. It was empty and likewise the fridge. This poor soul had not been eating. I washed out the mugs, dried them and put them into a cupboard and finished by cleaning the spilled coffee.

"Bob, you have cleaned that, you are a good man."

"Who me, I am not a good man I have done bad things in my life but only to bad people."

I helped her on with her coat and we walked down the stairs stepping out into the street and down towards a local Bistro and had a meal although Vesta only picked at hers. Throughout the conversation, it became clear that she had been left without money, food and the landlord had given her to the end of the month to be out of the flat. After about two hours, we left the Bistro and made our way back to her flat stopping at an all-night shop where I bought her some food and then stopped at a cash point where I withdrew some money for her. Whilst she was obviously grateful, it took a lot of persuasion on my part for her to take it.

"Bob, this the first time I have been out of the flat in about five weeks. I am frightened of people looking at me and thinking to themselves; look at her a prostitute. Before I came to this country, I could walk out of my house and speak to all my friends and wave to them across the road. None of them will ever speak to me again."

She started to cry again. I honestly did not know what to do. I was frightened to put my arm around her as I was sure the last thing she wanted was a man to touch her. I tried hard to lighten the conversation. As we continued down the road, I talked to her about Liz and the type of work she was doing, I suggested that this may be a group who could assist her through this difficult time and would get her away from Sergio should he ever come back. I hated lying to her about Sergio but what could I do. Tell her Sergio would never come back to rape and abuse her? I had no intention of doing that although inside me, I felt I wanted to tell someone.

Did I want to ease my conscience?

Chapter 51
More Money than I Had Ever Dreamt Of

It was a wet miserable day as I drove into the car park of Saint Anne's Manor on the outskirts of Wokingham. The trees were dripping wet and with every gust of wind, they dropped what seemed like a waterfall onto the drive below. As I walked past the reception area, I saw Frank sitting in the lounge he stood up as I walked over, we shook hands.

"Morning, Bob."

"Morning, Frank, and what a horrible morning weather wise it is."

"Not very good at all. Mind you it's better than when I left Hereford earlier on, it was blowing a gale and tippling it down. Fancy a coffee?"

"Yes, I'll call the waitress."

Indicating to the waitress standing next to the bar, she walked over and took our order, two cappuccinos and some biscuits.

"I have done the deal with my people and they were pleased with the metal and after taking their percentage and I got mine the total coming to you is."

He handed me an envelope; I opened it and read the contents, the money owed to me was nine million five hundred pounds sterling. I did a double take.

"This is after you and your people have taken the commission?"

"Yes, absolutely. There was a lot of metal there and it was of high quality. They were, and I might say I also was, very pleased to do business with you. They did mention if you have any similar products they would be pleased to do further business with you."

Fortunately, I was sipping my coffee and recovering from the shock of the amount of money; I knew it would be substantial but only about half of what I had seen on the paper. Frank looked at me.

"Everything okay?"

"Yes, fine, thanks for all you have done for me and others. I wish I could tell you."

"Bob, stop right there. I do not want to know I am sure you are doing all these things for the right reasons. Now let me tell you about payment. I have with me the total amount in Bearer Bonds in different amounts. They have been made out in your name and come from one of the top banks in Zurich. I would suggest that you visit Zurich with the one in the smaller amount and open a bank account in the smaller amount. They will not flinch at that amount and explain to them that you are doing business and anticipate there will be further and larger amounts paid into the account in the next few months. The amount you pay in over the next few months will be chicken feed to them."

With that, he handed me a large envelope.

"The bonds are inside. Why don't you visit the toilet and check them out, I'll wait here."

I took the envelope, made my way to the toilet, entered a cubicle and looked into the envelope. I counted them and sure enough, there were ten bonds to the value of nine million five hundred thousand pounds each with my name on them amongst the scrolled and very elaborate writing which was printed on what appeared to be parchment with some embossments in the centre. Each one was about the size of an A4 sheet of paper. I replaced them carefully into the envelope, left the cubicle and made my way back to the table and joined Frank.

"All okay?"

"Yes, fine, makes my pension from the Commissioner look rather silly."

"Well, I suppose you will put it to good use."

"Oh, yes I have plans for it and whilst on the subject I will be having access to a similar amount in a few months' time so I may have to call on your services again if that is okay by you."

"Yes, that is fine by me and I know it will be fine with my people."

I settled the bill; shook hands and we went our separate ways. My first stop was to Barclays Bank where I deposited the nine million pounds worth of bonds in my safe deposit box and removed a few thousand dollars which would help with my expenses in Switzerland.

On returning home, I telephoned Liz. She was not available but asked me to leave a message. I was becoming more and more concerned with Vesta's condition.

Eventually, Liz called back. I explained the situation that Vesta was in and asked if her people at the Salvation Army could assist; she said she would contact one of the officers and get back to me.

Within twenty minutes, the phone rang; it was Liz.

"Hi, Bob. I have spoken to a Major at the Salvation Army Headquarters in London. This officer has a meeting the day after tomorrow at The Regent Hall Corps in Regent Street; you remember I met you there a few months back."

"Yeah, the Rink."

"Correct, you're getting right into this, Bob; you'll be beating the big drum soon."

"It might surprise you, Liz. I was a drummer in the Boy's Brigade in Glasgow."

"Nothing about you surprises me."

"Oh, I don't know. I have a few hidden secrets."

"I bet you have, anyway if you could get to the Rink with Vesta the Major will speak to her at about three o'clock."

"Liz, you're a gem. I will be there with Vesta."

As soon as I finished the call, I telephoned Vesta. She sounded as if still shaken but agreed to meet with Liz and her friend. I agreed to meet her at the flat.

Chapter 52
Back to 'The Rink'

I arrived at Vesta's flat at about two o'clock she was waiting for me.

"Bob, thanks for doing this for me, I am frightened to meet these people are they good people?"

"Yes, the lady who is with Liz is a Salvation Army Officer. I do not know what you call the Salvation Army in your country but you have nothing to worry about."

"Bob, you have been so kind. Since I came to your country, I seem to have met so many bad people. I wonder every day what happened to all the girls I came here with?"

Sometimes I wonder myself why I ever got involved; all because I saw a book in a charity shop.

"Okay, Vesta let's go and get a taxi on the Kings Road."

After a few minutes, we were in a taxi and on our way to Oxford Street; I could sense the nervousness that Vesta was feeling. We pulled up outside the Salvation Army building paid the taxi driver and walked into the building and coffee shop, Liz was sitting in company with a very attractive woman aged about forty years dressed in a modern Salvation Army uniform of a white shirt with the wording of the Salvation Army embroidered on the front. On her shoulders were red epaulets her blouse collar was held together with an enamel clasp. Both Liz and the woman stood up and shook our hands, Liz spoke first.

"Hi, Bob, this is Major Beatie."

"Pleased to meet you, Bob, call me Jennifer. I have heard a lot about you from Liz."

I raised my eyebrows.

"This is Vesta."

They shook hands and sat down.

"I am Vesta. Bob has told me about Liz and your, is it church?"

"Yes, we are a church I am an Officer like a Minister or Vicar. My department's interest is in human trafficking and that is the acquisition of people by improper means that can be by means of force, fraud or deception with the sole aim of exploiting them. I would like to spend some time with you and hear what you have to say and if we can we will help you."

Vesta looked down at the table top and started sobbing; reaching out Liz held her hand. I felt as if I was intruding. God only knows how I, like so many police officers before me, had shared people's innermost secrets and could never reveal them.

This was so different; I had heard Vesta being raped and even she was not aware of this.

This for me was a heavy burden to carry.

"Who's for coffee?"

I took the order, walked over to the counter, collected the coffees and returned.

"Okay, coffee is up, there is milk and sugar on the way."

When I sat down, Vesta was telling how she had been enticed to come to England on the promise of lucrative work and how her life had fallen apart as soon as she arrived. The lady from behind the coffee shop counter arrived and put the sugar and milk on the table.

Jennifer looked up at me as I sat down.

"Vesta has started to tell me what is an only all too familiar story of her arrival here. Can I suggest that once we have had our coffee we retire to a more private area; I have asked the Corps Officer if we can use his room and he has agreed."

We finished our coffees. I looked at Jennifer.

"I have got a bit of shopping to do, so perhaps I can do that whilst you ladies carry on talking. Would that be suitable with you?"

"Yes, that's fine with us, Bob; shall we see you here in an hour?"

Jennifer smiled and gave a knowing wink, as if to say 'good man'.

I spent the next hour walking along Oxford Street; purchased a couple of shirts which I really didn't need and watched some very rich people spending money as if it was going out of fashion. Then I remembered I too was a millionaire.

Returning to the coffee shop, I waited for the ladies to return. It did not take long and within ten minutes, they arrived. The three of them looked a lot happier. Jennifer was first to speak.

"Well, Bob, we have had a good long chat and a prayer. I have spoken to my boss and there is a place available for Vesta at one of our safe houses outside London. Vesta says she would like to take up the offer and if you are agreeable, we would like to move her in there as soon as possible, say tomorrow. Would you be able to take her and her bags to The Salvation Army United Kingdom Headquarters one hundred and one Newington Causeway? Would you be able to bring her there tomorrow about three o'clock tomorrow afternoon? She seems to be frightened of a Russian man who was controlling her; his name is Sergio. Did you ever meet him, Bob?"

"No, from what I hear and read in the newspapers, he may have fled the country."

"Let's hope so. Liz has told me how you two met. I can't believe that was just by chance. You know Bob. God works in mysterious ways. God bless."

With that, we went our separate ways. On the way back in the car, Vesta broke down again. I held her hand as I drove.

"Bob, one night when I was in the flat, Sergio came to me with what he called a present. It was an underwear he made me wear. I said no and then he hit me many times and made me have sex. I tried to stop him but I could not; he was too strong. He ripped my Jesus from my neck and laughed. You know my Jesus is my Crucifix that my family gave me. He throws it on the floor. As he had sex. I could see it on the floor; my Jesus was looking at me. I say Jesus come and help me, but he did not. Bob, why did Jesus not help me?"

I could not answer that and most of all, I could not tell her I had heard it all on the tape recorder.

I dropped Vesta off at her flat with the promise of meeting her at two p.m. the following day.

Chapter 53
A Safe Haven?

I arrived on time outside Vesta's flat and walked up the stairs. As I did so, I saw her standing outside her door. As I got closer, I could see that her face was bruised with her left eye blackened and swollen.

"Vesta, what happened? Quick get indoors."

Ushering her indoors, I closed the door behind us.

"What on earth happened?"

She burst into tears and put her arms around me and through deep sobs, she tried to tell me.

"This morning at about eight o'clock, a man came to the door and when I answered, he said he was policeman and wanted to speak to a man called Sergio. He said he had come to take him to prison. I opened the door and he came in. I looked from the landing and he was standing downstairs with another man. They started to walk up the stairs and he took his badge out of his pocket. I said, come in. The man with the badge said we have come to take Sergio to prison, where is he? I said I did not know. Then the other man spoke and as soon as he did, I said to him you are Russian; you are not a policeman and with that, he slapped me on the face and pushed me onto the chair. He held me by the neck and started swearing and telling me they wanted Sergio and their gold. I kept telling them I know nothing; he kept slapping my face and then he put this pillow over my face and whispered into my ear saying I was going to die if I did not tell them. He then took pillow off my face and he takes gun from his jacket and holds it at my head. Then I hear policeman say put that thing away you will get us all nicked. I think that was the word. Policeman say fire that and every one in bloody flats hear it and the place will be full of 'armed response'. Russian man rips my top and tears my bra off and then pulls my tits very hard. I have much pain and I scream, policeman pulls him away and tells him to stop. Russian man says, she likes it Sergio tells me. Policeman says let's go, we will come back later and then they look in all things, you know searching, Yes?"

I helped Vesta to pack a couple of bags and made our way to my car. I opened the passenger door and indicated to Vesta to come to the car. She ran down the stairs and climbed into the seat. I closed her door, threw her bags into the rear of the car, got in and drove off towards South London and the U.K. Territory Headquarters of The Salvation Army Headquarters and a safe haven for Vesta.

As I drove into Sloane Square, we passed Peter Jones, the shop where we had met so many months before Vesta let out a scream.

"Oh my God, it's the policeman and the Russian."

She bent over double and I continued driving. Looking in my rear-view mirror, I saw the two figures walking away from us. I did not see the cop's face properly but I was sure I had seen him before.

"Vesta, you can get up now. They did not see you."

We arrived at the 'Sally Ann' and walked into the building where Vesta would start a new life and perhaps return home. It was time to say farewell. She hugged me, and what felt like ages she clung onto me. I was happy and felt I had done something good at last. My happiness was being spoiled by one thing going through my mind.

I was sure I knew the policeman who was outside Peter Jones with the Russian.

Chapter 54
Cashing In

I had never been to Geneva before so it was strange to me although most airports and hotels worldwide appear to be designed by the same architects. At home, I had booked my flights and the Hotel Des Bergues. On my arrival at Geneva Airport, I climbed into a taxi and was soon at this luxurious hotel. I had carried two of the bonds with me I immediately put them in my room safe. In the distance, I could view the Jet d'Eau, which is Europe's largest fountain. The information pack in the room credited it as reaching four hundred and sixty feet. I remained in the hotel and ate in my room.

The following morning, I travelled to the oldest bank in Geneva. Entering through the beautifully painted black doors each with large metal art work covered in gold leaf. The last time I had seen such quality paintwork was on the door at Ten Downing Street our Prime Minister's residence. On reaching the doors, they were opened by an immaculately dressed 'flunky' who directed me to a receptionist. This certainly was not your typical U.K. high street bank. I was seen by a delightful female who took all my details and then took me into an adjoining room where I was met by a well-dressed young man who went through all the bank's services. I explained that I was doing research for companies and would wish to deposit somewhere in the region of twenty million pounds over the next few months. The deposits would be in Bearer Bonds and handed him the Bonds I was carrying. He examined them and then excused himself and left the room with the Bonds. I glanced around the room I could have been sitting in the Victoria and Albert Museum in London. What looked like priceless paintings were hanging on the walls and for all I knew the furniture could be Chippendale. After a few minutes, the young man returned with some documents and asked me to produce my passport and any other documents to verify my address and status. I signed various documents and then he reached across the desk shook my hand and welcomed me as a valued customer of the bank. I received a receipt for the one and a half million pounds I had just deposited into MY account.

I left the bank and walked back to my hotel stopping at various bars on my way back.

Two days later, I returned to the bank and collected details of my account and then it was back to England and Wokingham, it could have been the other side of the moon; life was so different. I could not believe how easy it had been to open a Swiss Bank account.

Over the next few months, I returned to deposit the rest of the bonds. On one such visit, I consulted Solicitors with my details and instructed them as what to do in the event of my death, which of course is the only sure thing in life.

Life was pretty mundane after I deposited the remainder of the gold from my garage into the storage facility in Wokingham.

Two months later, Frank collected it and true to his word, I was paid in bonds and he took his commission as agreed. This of course meant more trips back and forward to Geneva and the bank where I was now becoming a familiar figure.

It was on my last flight home whilst waiting to collect my case that I saw a lady standing at the baggage carousel next to me she smiled and walked over to me.

"Hi, Bob."

It was Claire Johnson the wife of Chief Inspector Derek Johnson from Chelsea my mate from the old days. She put her arms around me and gave me a 'full on kiss'.

"Claire, how are you? I haven't seen you since your daughter's wedding. How are you?"

"I'm fine."

"And Derek?"

"We are divorced. It must be five years now. Did you know he is suspended at the moment?"

"No, what's that all about?"

"Long story, look here's my case."

She pulled it off the carousel with help from myself.

"Bob, I must rush. My daughter is outside with my granddaughter. Look, here's my phone number. Give me a ring. It would be good to meet up and talk over old times."

"I'll do that, bye."

She gave me a peck on the cheek and walked off pulling her Yves Saint-Laurent case behind her; as she did so she turned around and held her hand close to her ear in the shape of a phone and mouthed 'call me'.

I gave her the thumbs up and nodded. A rush of excitement rushed through my stomach, but not my loins as had happened long before she had been married.

I looked at her business card.

CLAIRE De-VALER

C.E.O

De-Valer Property Developers.

Ascot.

I knew she was well connected to some French geezer at the Battle of Hastings at least that was what she told me when we were courting what seemed to be in the long distant past.

Chapter 55
Memories

"De Valer Properties, how can I help you?"

I had taken the plunge. For years, I had wondered what had happened to Claire. I had lost contact with her.

"May I speak to Miss De Valer?"

"May I say who is calling?"

"Mister MacInally."

"One moment please."

I waited.

"I am putting you through now."

"Bob, how are you? Great to hear from you."

"I'm sorry I did not get a chance to talk properly to you at the airport."

"That's all right. I am sorry I had to rush off my driver was waiting for me to rush off to a meeting in London. How about we meet up for a drink?"

"Yeah, that would be great it would give us a chance to catch up in the last, what is it thirty years?"

"Yes, the last time I saw you must have been at my daughter's wedding and my dear husband had warned me not to speak to you. I got that he thought you were like him, trying to shag any girl who would let him into her knickers."

"Me?"

"Never mind 'me'. When can we meet up?"

"I am free most times."

"How about tomorrow night."

"That's fine by me. Do you know The Belvedere Pub at Ascot?"

"Yes, shall we say eight o' clock?"

"Yes, that's fine. See you then bye."

I arrived in the car park just as Claire was pulling in in her car; she stepped out and looked around as she set the alarm on the car. Looking across the car park, she waved as she spotted me. On reaching her, she gave me a peck on my cheek, stood back and smiled.

"Well, it's a long time since we were that close."

I returned the smile.

"If I was to tell you it was twenty-four years and three months would you believe me?"

She stared at me. I stared back. There was still some magic between us.

The waiter arrived and we ordered our food and some wine.

"Well, come on; tell me what you have been doing with yourself over all those years?"

What could I say?

Nothing much, left a murdering bastard to die in a tomb?

Blew up an evil raping killing Arab in Mallorca?

Fitted up a female who had cut up the body of an innocent girl and threw her head to the council tip?

Nicked some thieving slags gold from them?

"Nothing much. I have used the Commissioner's pension to have a few holidays and enjoying myself."

"That took you a while to answer, sorting out your story?"

She knew me too well.

"Is there a lady in your life?"

"No, not really. A couple of very good friends but nothing serious, how about you?"

"No."

"That sounded very definite?"

"Well, after what I went through with Derek, I don't think I could ever be serious with anyone again."

"What happened? I'm sorry I did not mean to pry."

Our food arrived. I raised my glass.

"To good friends."

"Good friends."

"You're not prying, but it is a long story."

"Carry on if you feel like it."

"It all started about ten years ago. My daughter was working in a Solicitor's office in the West End of London. One evening when she came home, I could tell she had been outside crying, I asked her over and over again what was the problem, I was sure it was an office problem. Eventually over a glass or two of wine, she blurted it out."

'Daddy's having an affair, I saw him with his lady in Selfridges Store he was buying expensive perfume for her. He did not see me and I asked Fiona from the office to stand next to them as I went outside. Apparently, Fiona came outside to my daughter and said he had bought an eighty odd pounds worth of perfume for her, gave it to her, kissed and walked off with his arm his arm around her to a local wine bar.'

"I had my suspicions for some time things were not right between us. One day, I was sorting out clothes for cleaning one morning and I found five hundred pounds in notes in the back pocket of his trousers it was in fifty-pound notes. I took them out and put them in my wardrobe. The trousers went to the cleaners and came back; he never even mentioned it was missing. Time went by and then he said we were going out for dinner with a guy he had been dealing with, a Russian, something to do with an international fraud or so he said. We went to a top restaurant in Mayfair. The Russian turned up with a lovely young foreign girl; she seemed to be scared stiff. I went to the toilet and whilst I was there she came in and looked at me and burst out crying. I hugged her and asked what was wrong. All she would say was 'mother', no more just 'mother'. I never got her name. The Russian guy was evil I think he was called Sergio. On the journey home, I said to Derek, I do not like your friend and as for that poor kid, she cried for her mother in the toilet. Derek turned around to me and said, 'I would not worry about her; she's only some Russian slag.' I lost my temper and said something like that Russian slag as you so nicely put it was crying for her mother in a poxy British toilet and this is the people you dine with. What the hell has happened to you, Derek? He turned to me and said if you don't like it, you can fuck off. I will be richer than you and your inherited money. He stopped the car and got out, took the keys out of the ignition and threw them on the floor and said do what you were told 'Fuck off.' I picked up the keys, got into the driver's seat and watched him as he got into a cab and was driven off."

"That does not sound like the Derek I knew. Mind you the job changes you. It's a couple of years back since I met him that was at Chelsea when he was telling me he had just finished a spell working in The Home Office."

She looked surprised.

"Home office, he was never at the Home Office. Sorry I'm jumping ahead of myself. He never came near the family or me since he got into that taxi. I eventually hired a private detective to find out as much as he could about Derek's activities. It transpired he had a number of women on the go and was spending money as if it was going out of fashion. He was meeting with Russian guys in Central London and as usual the evenings were spent with beautiful foreign girls. I changed the bank accounts and put them in my name. He could not get to my business accounts my solicitor saw to that. The divorce went through without any hiccups, he did not contest anything neither did he try to hit me for any more money than I had offered. It was thirty years of marriage put down to experience. I carried on with my business, which went from strength to strength and without the use of my so-called inherited wealth. Everything was doing fine until a few months ago when I received a phone call from a police officer from some special squad who wanted to come and see me at home. I agreed and she arrived two nights later. Her name was Chief Superintendent Margaret Cassidy."

Chapter 56
Filling in the Gaps

By the time, we had finished this part of the conversation. Our meals were getting cold, so we decided to have our coffee and liqueurs at one of the leather couches.

"I'm sorry if I am boring you, Bob, but it is so nice to have someone to talk to, I sort of buried myself in my business since the divorce."

"No, don't worry, you carry on. I am a good listener."

"Now where was I, oh, yes Margaret. I got to know her over the times she visited me. The first time she visited, she was with a Detective Sergeant from the Hampshire Police. I thought it was a little strange, her being from the Met. She started to talk to me and I found her to be a little evasive. It wasn't till some thirty minutes when I said to her, 'Margaret, I was married to a cop for too long so let's not beat about the bush, ask me whatever you want and I will help you in any way I can'."

"She looked into my eyes and without any hesitation, came straight out with it. Claire, did your husband ever discuss gold or gold bullion with you?"

That came as such a surprise to me; she could see I was visibly shocked, I immediately said, "No."

"She said, Russians?" I said right away yes and went on to tell her about the time I went to dinner with the little shit, and that was what I called him, 'a little shit', this seemed to impress her. She then went on to ask me to describe him. I did the best I could it was then she opened her laptop and showed me a number of what appeared to be passport pictures. When she reached the fourth or fifth picture, the little shit appeared.

I had no hesitation in picking him out. She explained that she had an interest in this man and was aware that my former husband had been associating with him and others. It was at this point, I told her about the private investigator I had hired. She seemed interested and I left the room, returning with my folder of the work done by the P.I. She thumbed through the report and photographs stopping at a couple of pictures and pointing something in them to her colleague who nodded and made some notes and then returned the pictures to his boss. She read through more of the file and looked up at me, her face was a lot more serious looking. 'Claire, when was the last time you saw the Private Investigator, Mister Logan?' I told her it was about nine months before and asked why? She looked at me and paused.

"He was found dead in a country park near Wokingham."

"I asked how did he die?"

"Two bullets in the back of his head as he sat in his car."

I could not believe it; he was such a nice guy. I believe he was married with two children. I then asked her in what country park had he been found?

"The Black Swan, why do you ask?"

Chapter 57
Bob I'm in Deep Trouble

It was closing time when we left the Belvedere Arms pub, I had only had a couple of glasses of wine and felt fine to drive, it was a clear summer's night as I made my way towards Wokingham. As I reached The Ship Public House, a guy on a bicycle came out of the pub car park and cycled into the side of my car. He fell to the ground and lay still his bike on top of him. A few 'pissed up' locals ran over and lifted his bike off him as I tried to get out of the car.

"Stay there, mate. You're pissed."

I had to agree with the kind-hearted citizen who was looking after the cyclist, but I was wrong which was confirmed as the next drunk spoke.

"He was knocking back pints in the pub; they should hang bastards like you."

Then another guy whispered into my ear.

"I would piss off if I was you the 'Old Bill' are on their way." No sooner had he spoken than two police cars closely followed by an ambulance arrived at the scene and were welcomed with cheers from the drunken rabble surrounding my car. The cyclist was now on his feet claiming he had never seen the bicycle before.

I was ushered into the rear seat of the police car and driven off.

"I will take you to the local nick where we will breath test you away from this bunch of 'local travellers'. The landlord has banned them from the pub but they come in 'mob handed', order rounds of drinks and don't pay for them, they are nothing but trouble."

With that, I was taken into the police station and breath tested for alcohol, finger printed and a sample of my DNA was taken.

"The breath test was negative, sir; we will let you out with your car in a couple of minutes when the van brings in some of the drunks from the scene of your accident. I will give you the details of the 'pisshead' who rode into you and you can pass it onto your insurers, but to tell you the truth, you do not have a hope in hell of getting anything from him."

I left the police station as the drunken cyclist was being taken out of the police van together with the bicycle, which apparently had been stolen from outside the pub.

Just another day in the life of the poor 'British Bobby'.

Six months passed with very little happening. I spoke to Liz a few times and had a couple of meals with Claire but I'm sad to say all the old magic had gone. As she said, I had changed and put on weight. I did not have the heart to tell her she was getting wrinkled.

Sitting at home reading Alan Whicker's book that I had bought, what seemed like so many years before my telephone rang, with my usual thought of 'who rings at this time of night, I answered.

"Bob MacInally."

"Hi, Bob. Derek Johnson. How are you doing?"

"I'm fine. I understand you have a bit of grief."

"Yeah, the word soon gets about. It was that I wanted to speak to you about. I would like an ear to listen to my problems. I suppose you know I am suspended at the moment; I would like to have a 'meet' if you are agreeable?"

"Yes, sure when were you thinking of? But just one thing, where did you get this number from?"

"It's a bit of a long story. I'll tell you all about it when me meet."

"Fine, when?"

"Well, the sooner the better. I think I'm going to be 'fitted up' by someone in the job who has got it in for me, the job's not what it was. You just can't trust anyone these days, sell their grannies for the next rank."

"So, Derek when do you fancy meeting?"

"How about tomorrow?"

"That's okay by me. Where?"

"Do you know the Castle Hotel opposite Windsor Castle in Windsor?"

"What about twelve noon?"

"That's fine by me."

"See you then."

I hung up, what the hell did he want?

Chapter 58
A Bit of Weeding

I was in plenty of time when I arrived at the hotel. Sitting in the lounge, I stared out at the cobbled approach to the castle entrance with the tourist mouths opening as they stared in awe at the majestic building. After a few minutes, Derek arrived. He had lost a lot of weight since I saw him last in Chelsea Police Station, he looked about and eventually spotted me, walking over he reached out his right hand.

"Hi, Bob, how are you doing?"

"I'm fine, and you?"

"Well, I've had better years. The bastards at the big house have suspended me without a shred of evidence against me. I'm no longer with Claire. It just was not working out. She was playing about and when I challenged her about it she of course denied it. I've been living like a hermit for years."

The waiter walked over and tried to take our order.

"Coffee, Derek?"

"No, I'll have Scotch, if that's okay with you?"

"Yeah okay and I will have another coffee."

Before the waiter had time to write down the order, Derek interrupted.

"Make that a double."

He smiled at me, bent forward and in a whispered voice started to talk.

"Bob, I need a big favour and if you feel you cannot help, I will understand but for reasons that will become obvious, I would not want this to go any further. Yes?"

The waiter arrived and served the drinks together with the bill. Derek stopped talking until he left.

"I suppose you heard all about the big gold blag at the Cargo depot at Heathrow."

"Yeah, forty or fifty million pounds?"

"And the rest. Well, we were aware that the villains had split it into smaller packages making it much easier to handle. They were moving it about in large fire extinguishers that could be barrowed into premises without any person taking any notice. They even had a van done up as a fire extinguisher company, it was all large industrial extinguishers they were using, you know like they use in harbours and private airports. If they got a pull by the police, it was 'all okay', I mean what 'old bill' is going to start screwing the tops off fire extinguishers. Well, I got a bit of information about a load they were moving. Call it silly or whatever, I gave some Russian guys the nod of the times and movement. Believe it or not, there was only one person moving the van. The villains thought it looked more kosher and in fact, it did. The driver was kitted out in proper overalls. When the load was going through Hampshire, a team of Russians pulled the van over and had the driver away. I never heard what they did with him.

"My little Russia 'snout' thought they had 'topped' him and the van had gone to a breaker's yard and been crushed. The 'snout' got the job of moving and storing it, after that it became a bit of a mystery. You see I didn't realise my 'snout' had diplomatic immunity, being involved with the Russian Embassy. The next time I saw any of the gold was in a Diplomatic flat in Mayfair. They had laid on two little 'dolls' for me for a couple of nights. They were Eastern Europeans aged about eighteen years, 'they went through the cards' with me. My man came back and told them to piss off and he laid on another one for me. I went out for dinner with her and my man, I took Claire and he pretended the little one was with him. The silly little cow started to cry in the toilet with Claire. The shit almost hit the van on the way home. I thought she had told Claire the whole story and it was at that point I pissed off from Claire. I 'weeded some of the gold bars'. My luck changed at that time, the Russian 'legged it' with the rest of the gold, they think he is in Northern Cyprus, but they will find him. He will be topped; you don't fuck about with these people.

"That was where that silly cow Claire almost dropped me in the shit. She's only gone and got a P.I. to follow me, almost dropped me in the shit, silly cow.

"This is where I need a 'leg up'. I will ask you straight out can you store six bars of gold bullion for me, they are worth about two and a half million pounds? You are welcome to half."

"I can't imagine gold is the easiest thing to sell."

"Don't worry, I'll give the name of a 'Jew Boy' in Hatton Garden who will take all you can give him as long as it is in small quantities. Are you up for it?"

"When were you thinking of doing it?"

"The sooner the better. I think that Margaret Cassidy is going to try and feel my collar soon on some trumped up charge. She thinks I was copping a few bob off a little drug dealer in Chelsea, it'll never stick but if she spins my place and finds the gold I'm in the brown stuff."

"I have a place where I can store it but I would want to collect it away from there. Do you know the 'Park and Ride at the Winnersh Cinema Complex just off junction ten on the M. Four?"

"How about in two days' time, Friday?"

"Yes, that suits me, let's say three p.m. what car will you be driving?"

"I'll be in my red B.M.W Estate car."

"Okay, three o'clock Friday."

We shook hands and went our separate ways.

Chapter 59
A Matinee Performance

It was about one o'clock as I pulled into the Oracle shopping centre car park in Reading town centre. A ten-minute drive from the Multiplex Cinema Complex Car Park where I had arranged to meet Derek Johnson, I had time to spare. It was a short walk to the Park and Ride Point where the bus would take me back to the area where I hoped my plan would fall into place. I walked to the bus pickup point and got on pulling on my baseball cap as I did so. I sat at a window seat and watched as the bus travelled down the bus lane from Reading and into the car park where I got off and made my way into the cinema foyer which was identical to these buildings over the country and no doubt worldwide. Ordering a carton of popcorn, I made my way to the windows at the entrance. The people attending the Matinee performance seemed to be made up of pensioners waiting for their discounted tickets. At two fifty-five, I saw a red B.M.W. estate car drive into the car park and stop in a parking space well away from other cars. It was Derek Johnson driving. He sat in the car for about five minute and then got out and walked to the front and rested on the bonnet. Taking a packet of cigarettes from his pocket, he lit a cigarette inhaling it and holding the smoke in his lungs until he slowly exhaled it. Finishing the cigarette, he flicked the end into the bushes and started to walk up and down the car park. A car pulled up nearby and two men walked over to him; I had seen this type of walk before their arms were outstretched holding wallets in their hands. To me, it was obvious they were plain clothes police officers and were introducing themselves to Johnson. He stood still arms outstretched. It was obvious he was arguing with them. One officer was holding his hand out very obviously asking Johnson for his car keys; it appeared he was not co-operating. Another two people walked over towards him. One was Chief Superintendent Cassidy, Johnson held out his hand as if wishing her to shake his. She refused. He stood still, hands turned upwards as he shook his head and reached through the open driver's door and appeared to remove the ignition keys. He walked to the rear of the car and pressed the key fob. The boot lid opened, as it did so Johnson leant forward and reached into the boot and suddenly spun around, pistol in hand letting off four rounds as he did so. Two of the male officers fell to the ground. No sooner did this happen when the doors of a Ford Transit Van burst open and four heavily armed police officer dressed in black overalls with army style combat helmets jumped out screaming 'armed police drop your weapon'. Johnson was shouting "you bastard Cassidy" as he stumbled backwards pointing his handgun at Margaret Cassidy; she spun around and fell to the ground.

Johnson's body lifted off the ground ever so slightly and turned backwards, he was hit by a hail of bullets from the armed police officer's weapons. The officers ran over to the body, which was giving jerking movements; blood was oozing out of it and on to the black Tarmac. The body laid lifeless. Suddenly, there was an unearthly silence, which was broken by the ear-piercing sounds from the sirens of more emergency vehicles racing to the scene. Pensioners who had been out for an afternoon at the discounted matinee were now 'extras' in this real-life drama.

Ambulance crews were running to the scene their emergency bags slung over their shoulders and were soon bent over the two injured officers who were stretchered off the scene and put into two separate ambulances that raced off to a local hospital.

Police using blue and white plastic tapes cordoned off the scene.

It was time for me to get out of the area. I managed to get onto the last bus back into reading paid for my parking time and drove home.

I kept thinking to myself I wished I had not made the anonymous call to Margaret's office telling the staff about the meeting.

Chapter 60
Good News Bad News

As soon as I arrived home, I switched on the television. The news channels were all focused on the shooting of three police officers in Winnersh. Most of them were having difficulty on trying to explain where Winnersh was located some were saying 'close to Henley on Thames' others were saying it was 'close to Windsor Castle' the one that got the closest to its location said it was about five miles east from the town of Reading.

One of the channels went over to 'the scene of the shootings'. It showed a general view of the car park with police scientists walking about the area in their white forensic suits.

A female reporter was doing her 'bit to camera' adjusting her earpiece as she spoke.

"I am at the scene in Winnersh in the Thames Valley area. A police spokesman has told me that this was a well-planned operation to arrest a member of one gang suspected of taking part in what has become known as the Gold bullion job at Heathrow Airport."

She then adjusted her earpiece again.

"I am just being told there will be a press conference at Loddon Valley Police station in two hours' time."

I made my way to the kitchen and made a cup of coffee. As I stood drinking and looking out of the window, I was in a world of my own. Thoughts raced through my mind. *Did I lead that Margaret into a trap? Should I have given her office more information?* But how was I to know that Johnson would have been 'tooled up' at the meet and most of all how would I have ever thought he would shoot his colleagues?'

I finished my coffee and sat down in front of the television. The reporters were having a hard time trying to put together the story which was only a few hours old. Suddenly, their efforts were interrupted by an announcement from the studio.

We are now going over to Loddon Bridge Police Station in the Thames Valley Region where a police conference is about to commence. The picture changed to a view of an empty table with a row of chairs behind it. Rows of microphones covered the table. A male reporter came into shot asking 'Keith' if the sound level was okay. There was no reply as the Police Press officer led in a number of senior officers.

"Good afternoon, ladies and gentlemen. I am Brian Mann the Thames Valley Police Press Liaison Officer let me introduce you to." He then went on to introduce various officers sitting at the table, stating there would be time for a few questions at the end of the conference. He then introduced the Detective Chief Superintendent.

"Good evening, ladies and gentlemen. I am Detective Superintendent Robert Bryson Mackie of the Thames Valley Police. This afternoon, an operation was carried out by officers of the Metropolitan Police under the Command of Detective Superintendent Margaret Cassidy supported by of SO Nineteen, The Met's Firearms Department. At approximately three o' clock this afternoon, two CID officers from the Met approached a red B.M.W. Estate car in the car park of the Multiplex Cinema in Winnersh. The driver, who was standing outside the car, was spoken to by the two officers. I would like to point out, at this time; his identity was known to the officers. He took the officers to the rear of his car, opened the boot and without warning shot the two officers who fell to the ground. These two officers are currently in the Royal Berkshire Hospital being treated for their injuries which I am pleased to say are not life threatening, their relatives have been informed and will be with them very shortly. With regards to the other person, he was shot by officers from SO Nineteen Branch of the Met who had been secreted nearby, he died at the scene. This man has been named as Derek Johnson a CID officer with the Metropolitan Police. At the time of this incident, he had been suspended from duty for some months. This matter is now in the hands of the Independent Police Complaints Commission. Thank you."

The questions from the press flew fast and furious.

Why was Johnson suspended?

Did he shoot his colleagues with a police weapon?

There is a rumour gold bullion was found in the car?

Did the Met inform Thames Valley Police about this operation?

Why is Margaret Cassidy not at this press conference?

They all received the same answer. "This is a matter for the Independent Police Complaints Commission."

The conference soon finished. It was very clear the local police were not too happy about the day's events.

The next day, the newspapers were full of the story.

I tried phoning Claire but as I expected, her phone was switched off. It was a week later when she phoned me; she was very upset.

"Bob, no doubt you have heard the news about Derek. The kids are taking it really bad, particularly when they see the headlines 'bent cop shoots mates'. It is so hard whatever got into him. I'm sure it was these bloody Russians that turned him in. When I think of what he said to me in the car 'I will have more money than you', it is so sad he was straight when I first knew him. That's not the worst of it, Margaret Cassidy has been to see me, that gun he used was the same one used to kill the P.I. I had used to follow him. I feel terrible if only I had not hired the poor man he would be alive today, at least the two other guys he shot have been discharged from hospital. Did you know he tried to kill Margaret, she said that as he pointed the gun at her he said 'this is all you fault'. What a mess, how did it get to this state?"

Chapter 61
Coroners Court

I was some months later when the report from the Coroner's court appeared in the national newspapers. Various people gave evidence of attending the scene of the shooting. The two officers gave their evidence of how Johnson seemed affable and had in fact joked with the about them being off their beat, a reference to them being in another police area. They both said it was not until they asked him to open the boot of the car that he became aggressive and refused to say who he was waiting for. After some more chat, he reached into the car and said okay no problem. He took out the ignition key and an alarm key fob. He pressed the fob and the boot opened and slowly lifted. It was at this point he shot forward and reached into the boot. Within what seemed a split second, he pulled a pistol from the boot and shouted 'bastards'. Both officers said they were hit with one bullet each. The bullets had lodged in their shoulders as they fell to the ground and they feared they were going to be killed.

The next officer to give evidence was Detective Superintendent Margaret Cassidy, who after taking the oath said her office had received information from an anonymous telephone call to her office. She said that she was very wary of this type of call. The call had described the car and said it would be carrying gold ingots. She then said, "I was aware that Inspector Johnson had been having unofficial dealings with Russian gang members and this was why he had been suspended from duty. I was also aware Johnson was the owner of a red BMW Estate car and I had the registration number of it." It was when this car arrived at the location I realised the information was more than likely to be correct. I watched his activities from a police observation vehicle. He got out of the car lit up a cigarette and stood at the front of the car, I instructed two officers to introduce themselves as police officers. There was some form of conversation taking place I left the observation vehicle and spoke to Johnson I tried to calm him down he was becoming very argumentative, he seemed to be seeing reason and removed his car keys from the ignition reaching through the driver's open window. He then walked towards the rear of his car pressing the key fob as he did so causing the boot to open. He lunged forward into the boot and spun around, gun in hand and shot my two officers. I dived to the ground looking at Johnson as he pointed his gun towards me shouting something like 'you bastard caused this' and in the same split second he fell backwards as the rounds from the firearms officer's weapons hit him in the chest. A moment later, I turned around as I lay on the ground getting onto my knees. I looked towards him. I could see he was dead. I instinctively kicked the gun away from him. Assisting myself to get up from the ground, I held onto the boot of the car as I did so I could see a number of gold ingots inside.'

She continued her evidence.

'Subsequent tests on the pistol used by Johnson to shoot the officers proved identical to the gun used to a kill a private investigator some months earlier. Forensic tests carried on Johnson's car and the car in which the Private Investigator died prove conclusively that Johnson shot and killed the investigator by shooting him twice in the back of his head.'

Evidence was taken from the firearms officers and after two days, the case finished with all three offices being commended by the coroner for their bravery.

And yet another chapter in my life ended. I was happy it seemed to be finished and to be perfectly honest I was beginning to think I had enough of the life and job I had loved. Besides that, I hadn't been feeling too well and decided to take things easy.

Months passed and I was still in contact with Liz and Claire.

Chapter 62
I Did Not Expect That, Then Again Who Does?

"Mister MacInally?"

I stood up and raised my hand. The nurse looked at me.

"Doctor Cole will see you now."

I followed her past the desk and into a small area outside a door marked Doctor David Cole. Oncologist.

The nurse knocked on the door and opened the door without waiting for a reply. She handed the doctor a manila-coloured folder with lots of paper inside.

"Thank you, nurse. Ah, Mister MacInally, how do you prefer to be addressed?"

"Just call me Bob. I've been called a lot worse in my time."

"Yes, I see you were a police officer, retired now?"

"Yes."

"I have the results of your tests and they show a number of cancerous cells in your blood and as a result of that I would like to carry out some further tests and depending on the results we may have to carry out an exploratory operation. I have checked the diary and we can see you this Thursday."

The rest is history. They discovered advanced Liver Cancer had spread and in the nicest way possible they told me I about six months to live.

I walked back to my car and found a parking ticket for being twelve minutes over time.

I took the ticket off the windscreen and sat in my car and read it again. I started to shout and hit my steering wheel I was so angry.

Twelve fucking minutes. I've got at the most one hundred and eighty days to live. What you going to do then, give me more fucking tickets for not paying this. Bastards, I burst out crying uncontrollably.

The Parking Attendant knocked on my window. I wound it down and looked at her. She could see I was crying.

"I'm sorry, sir, but you were twelve minutes over time."

"Twelve fucking minutes, do you know how precious twelve minutes are to me?"

"Well, sir, if you pay within thirty days, the sixty pounds' penalty will be reduced to thirty. So don't cry, sir, it is not as bad as it seems. You have got plenty of time."

I looked up at her and laughed.

"Whoopee do, one hundred and eighty fucking days!"

Chapter 63
Countdown

I decided to get on with things the best I could. I withdrew everything from the safe deposit box at the bank and changed the dollars into pounds and closed down my accounts. When I got home, I counted the money I had left. There was about three hundred and fifty thousand pounds. I divided it into various amounts and put it into envelopes. I was getting some satisfaction, as I would be bringing happiness to some people with the 'slags' money.

The phone rang it was Liz.

"Hi, Bob, we have not spoken for some time. How are things?"

"Oh, well things have been better."

"Why what's wrong, things can't be that bad, surely?"

"Don't call me Shirley."

"Same old Bob always joking. So, what's wrong?"

I went through everything with her.

"I am off this Saturday. Is it okay for me to come over and visit?"

"Yes, sure whatever time suits you."

"Any time suits me."

"I'll try and make it for three, okay?"

"Fine. I will see you then."

I could feel myself getting weaker each day but was helped greatly by the 'girls' from Macmillan Nurses Cancer support.

Saturday came and Liz arrived and told me all, the latest news from the safe house. She brought me a letter from Vesta who was still at the Salvation Army's safe house and was shortly moving to live in Australia.

We talked for ages and much to my surprise, she asked if she could pray with me. I nodded and she took hold of my hands and we shut our eyes. She prayed so quietly. She read from a Salvation Army songbook she had with her. I would never forget the words.

'There'll be no sorrow in God's tomorrow,
There'll be no sadness, doubts or fears,
There'll be no sorrow in God's tomorrow,
For he will wipe away all tears.'

We hugged each other for some time we barely spoke and then she left.

I don't why she chose that reading but it got to me and brought me some comfort.

Liz visited me many times over the next few weeks. Boy, whatever she had found in life, I wanted some of it.

The most unexpected call came from Margaret Cassidy.

"Bob, it's Margaret Cassidy. I was talking to Claire yesterday and she was telling me you were not keeping too well. I was wondering if I could pop over to see you, one pensioner to another?"

"Have you retired now?"

"Yes, it's six months now and I am enjoying every minute."

"Yes, if you want to come over you are more than welcome."

It was two days later when she arrived.

"Well, Bob, this has been a long time in coming. I have admired what you did in the job. It was such a pity that you left and you did good work when you left. The job could do with some good old-fashioned police work, as you know there are too many slags walking out of court and they are as guilty as hell. Now they are appealing on some technicality after they have been banged up for ten years or more. The country has had enough of it. That Derek Johnson was a bad one. I knew it for years but no one would listen.

"I was given an old case to look at, a slag by the name of Megan Jones you may remember she had cut up a poor kid's body and dumped her head in a council tip. She decided to appeal saying she had been fitted up. The file arrived on my desk with some DNA samples from some guy who had been nicked in Wokingham suspected of being pissed when driving. They seemed to think that DNA matched DNA found on plastic bags found in the back of a mini bus she had been driving. Her prints and DNA were all over the exhibits inside the bags, which by the way were accidentally destroyed by me. It's the pressure of work that causes this type of things to happen. I am sure you will understand."

She got up to leave.

"Bob, there is a Russian guy called Segio Barakova. He has gone missing. He was the scumbag who was trafficking young girls from Eastern Bloc countries. I don't suppose you have any idea what happened to him, the 'old bill' are still looking for him?"

"Well, if you should be talking to them, tell them not to bother taking handcuffs… Take flowers instead."

She looked at me, shook her head and smiled.

"Bob MacInally, you are an awful man."

And with that, she left.

Chapter 64
Liz's Tale

It was only three months after Bob had been diagnosed with cancer that he passed away. I visited him many times during this period. He never complained once and pulled my leg on many occasions about; 'the Lord working in mysterious ways'. He would often say, 'oh well I might get the chance to speak to him about that any time now'.

Twice he asked me to pray with him. I read a passage of Scripture to him on one occasion it was from Mathew's Gospel.

Come to me, all who are weary and burdened,
and I will give you rest.

He looked at me with tear filled eyes and quietly whispered,
'That's one hell of a promise'. He was dozing off as I said to him,
"It worked for me, a young 'prossi' from Liverpool."
The next day when I visited, he took four large envelopes from his locker. One was addressed to me another, was for Claire Johnson and had:
'Give this to the kids; it will be a little start in life for them'.
Written on the outside of another read;
'For Margaret Cassidy, to be given to the Metropolitan Police Widow and Orphans Fund'.
He looked at me as he handed me a hand-written list and said:
"When I fall off my perch, phone these people on the list and tell them when the funeral will be and after it's over, hand out the envelopes to them."
Three weeks later, I was sitting next to his bed. I could see he had at the most one day to go. He was in a deep sleep; his breathing was becoming 'laboured'.
His eyes ever so slowly opened as he tried to focus on me. He barely lifted his right hand and through his dry lips, he tried to whisper 'Liz.'

I said I'm here Bob and took hold of his hand and held it. He started to whisper, "There'll be no sorrow in God's tomorrow."

It was too much of a struggle for him; I bent down next to his ear and whispered as I finished it for him;

'There'll be no sadness, doubts or fears,

There'll be no sorrow in God's tomorrow,

For he will wipe away all tears.'

There was a gentle smile as the grip on his hand eased off.

Bob the good policeman had left this worldly place.

I cried a lot for this man who had been like a father to me and had replaced the one I had never had. I remembered how once Bob had told me how some policemen had frequently developed friendships with people who had a rough deal in life; he had certainly been a comfort to me.

The funeral took place two weeks later, about fifty people attended and a retired policewoman gave the eulogy. She introduced herself as Margaret Johnson and spoke highly of Bob; the unorthodox policeman as she described him. She told how they had courted at an early age and how he found his new love, the police service and they went their different ways and how Bob would have stayed 'married' to the police if it hadn't been for the bullets from a bank robber's pistol that caused him to retire early from the job he loved. She described how they met by chance at Heathrow Airport and had managed to catch up on the missing years but alas time had taken its toll and they both had changed, but she felt there was still a little flame still burning between them.

When I returned home, I opened the envelope he had given me. There were about fifty thousand pounds in U.S. dollars. There was a dry fusty smell from the notes as if they had been stored in some cave or some place for years. I have carried on my life as usual helping the girls who had been subjected to human trafficking. I often give thanks to the Lord for Mary the Salvation Army Officer who helped me when I needed it most; and Bob who helped to keep me on the straight and narrow. I often find myself singing to myself Bob's favourite song and I know for Bob the tears have been wiped away.

Chapter 65
Eighteen Months Later

The International Headquarters
The Salvation Army 101 Queen Victoria Street
London England.

An officer walked along the corridor on the fifth floor. She had come to see her boss who was sitting at his desk with his office door open.

"Good morning, Colonel."

"Ah, Beata, good morning. Come in. What brings you here?"

"Well, I require some advice; this letter came in from solicitors in the City of London to be precise. I don't think it is something I can deal with; it relates to a Will from one of their late clients in Europe. It would appear he was a UK National and prepared his Will with them some time ago. The solicitors said it was his request for all his funds which were deposited in an off shore bank some years ago should come to the 'Army'. They say the account lay dormant for years and has accumulated a considerable amount of interest during this time. He has stated that the following conditions must be fulfilled.

"'One.' The money must go to the work of the 'Army'.

"'Two.' This money where possible, should go to the fight against human trafficking.

"'Three.' The name of the person who is donating should not be divulged outside the senior people in the 'Army' who are dealing with the matter. He then goes on to say that his name can be disclosed to any government having cause to deal with it in cases where money laundering is suspected."

The Colonel looked up over his spectacles.

"What a strange request although we have had similar in the past. By the way, Beata, what sum of money are we talking about here?"

"It is several millions of pounds."

There was a short silence.

Rising slowly from his chair and resting his spectacles on the desk, he stared at Beata as he held out his hand to take the letter.

"Did I hear you correctly?"

He took the letter, copies of the Will and bank details and studied them for about five minutes.

"We without a doubt will have to pass this onto the Legal and Legacy Department and no doubt this will have to be fully passed to the Government Department who deal with Money Laundering."

The correspondence was passed on through the appropriate channels; after eighteen months, all the documents arrived back and were given the seal of approval by all the departments involved.

A meeting was called in the Rotunda the board room at I.H.Q. a Colonel addressed the meeting. He explained the legacy, the largest ever and how it would be used to the benefit and improvement in the fight against human trafficking.

A hand was raised by one of the officer's present.

"Are we aware of any illegal connections to this money?"

The Colonel standing rested his hands on the table and looked at those present.

"I suppose you mean is it 'tainted' money? May I remind you the answer The Founder gave when he arrived in New York over a hundred and twenty years ago. The Press fired many questions at him, and when asked would he accept 'tainted money' he replied the only thing about 'tainted money' it ain't enough!"

He then went on to say, "I would take anyone's money and wash it in the tears of widows and orphans and lay it on the altar of benevolent effort for the good of the great cause."

I see the benefactor had one request that he would like two rooms or buildings where possible to be named, 'MARY' and 'LIZ'.

With that, he closed the file and asked the assembled company to join him in prayer.

Closing the file, he put it on the desk as the assembled company joined him in prayer.

His hand rested on the cover of the file covering a series of reference numbers but leaving the last part of the reference uncovered; it read.

R.W.W.M.

Acknowledgments

Mortin Short (Thames Television)

Wellingtons Goldsmith Silver Smith (Wokingham, England)

Country Cleaners and Locksmiths (Wokingham, England)

Jay Design and Print (Wokingham, England)

Bill Fairweather Regent Palace Hotel (London, England)

Gaynor H20 (Wokingham, England)

ACORN (Hereford, England)

THE GUN STORE (Las Vegas)

Gregory and Steven (my sons)

Catherine (my sister)

David Woodland (Spain)

Tony and Maggi (Wokingham)

Margaret Meldrum (London)

All friends in Puerto Pollensa over the past 35 years (Mallorca)

Don Giovanni Riverside Restaurant (Wokingham)

Rossini Restaurant. Ristorante Italiano (Wokingham)